THE DUMNONIAN COMPASS

S B POSTLEWHITE

For my children Luke and Caitlin, who grew-up alongside Darcy. All my love, now and always.

My husband Andy, who holds my hand and my heart.
My friend, Sue Osborne, and my Dad, Vic Clement, who were early editors and critics on this project.

Sharon Irving, who shared my Cornwall solar eclipse adventure. BFF.
Special Friends who have encouraged me along the way. Too many to name but too important to leave out. Thank you...

CHAPTER ONE

JAMMING TRAFFIC

Darcy Bennet, well actually Darcy Elizabeth Bennet, owing to her mother's obsession with all things Jane Austen, has the most embarrassing parents on the planet. They're both archaeologists. That's not embarrassing, so far, in fact, sometimes it's even exciting. It's just that they dress, well, it can only be described as in the same 'Austen' vibe. Ruffed, blousy shirts and three-quarter length trousers like something caught in a time warp since the end of the 1780s. Sometimes Darcy wished, you know how it is, that the ground would open and swallow her up. Or that she was invisible and that no one would see her with them. She was busy thinking this to herself when she remembered she should be grateful. She could have been called 'Marianne' or even 'Willoughby', but luckily those were the names of the dogs.

The only time that Darcy's mother and father act in a way that she would describe as normal is when they are working. For all their weirdness and the terrible dress sense, Darcy does like them. They are fun, but they are completely obsessed with people who died hundreds of years ago. Sometimes Darcy thought that if she were a two-hundred-year-old dead person, they might notice her.

Today is Darcy's fifteenth birthday. It's August, and the family is off to Cornwall on holiday. They had holidayed there for the first-time last year, and Darcy had persuaded her parents that it had been the best holiday she'd ever had. That was true. She also told them how much she wanted to go back there. As it was her birthday while they were to take their next holiday, Darcy thought it would be, well, 'nice,' if she were the one to choose where that holiday was to be, as part of her birthday present. Thank goodness they didn't know the real reason.

So here they are, stuck in traffic, with Darcy remembering back to how it all started, almost exactly one year before...

1999 is significant for more than just being the end of a millennium. A total solar eclipse was expected in southern England, and the Bennet's were attempting the drive to Cornwall.

'Will this ever end?' said Pippa, 'I don't know how much more I can take.'

'What were you expecting?' said Tom.

He looked at his wife. A pain pulsed at the back of his eyes. He flinched. The pain had been getting increasingly worse for the last hour. Tom reached up and rubbed his left temple with the tip of one finger, turned, and squinting again at the road ahead, said,

'The eclipse is only two days away; it was always going to be busy.'

Tom and Pippa Bennet are the type of people that if you saw them in the street, you would have to give them a second glance, just to check that what you thought you saw the first time, was actually what you saw. Tom, in the driver's seat, was sporting a baggy florescent orange T-shirt. It clashed violently with the red-brown hair that fell messily onto his shoulders. His long legs were encased in the scruffiest pair of jeans imaginable. On his feet were the only new piece of clothing that he had bought in the last year, green flip-flops. Although at first appearances, you would say Tom Bennet looked eccentric, he has a face that lights up when he smiles, which is often, and deep green eyes that belie a gentleness. Meaning before long, and probably against your natural inclination, you would find yourself liking him.

Pippa's dress sense is much like her husbands. Loud and with a blatant disregard for current fashion trends. On this day she is wearing a long green maxi type dress that falls loosely to her ankles and has large tie-died circular patterns all over it. Perched on her head is a wide-brimmed straw hat, under which her black hair is shimmering in the sunshine streaming through the car window. She looks to all intents and purposes, sitting in the passenger seat of their old Ford, like a serene, oversized leprechaun. Or that's what is on Darcy's mind, as she listens to the conversation her parents are having in the front seats of the car.

It is one of Darcy's goals in life to act and dress as different from her parents as is humanly possible.

'How far do we still have to go?' she asked them.

She looked from the book she was reading to study her own clothes critically. Tidy jeans, trainers and a white T-shirt; *normal*, she thought.

'We're only just coming into Exeter,' said Tom, 'I would say we have at least another hour of this.'

Darcy let her breath out slowly. It hissed through the gaps in her teeth.

Why did they have this crazy idea to come all the way down here this week of all weeks? It's probably the busiest Cornwall has ever been.

As Darcy thought this, the answer was already forming itself.

It's that crazy obsession they've got with all things ancient and dead. If I made the rules, I would make sure that when people go on holiday, they do something completely different from what they do for the rest of the year.

She glared at the back of their heads, then buried herself once again in the book.

Although Darcy was grown up for an almost fourteen-year-old, she still found it very difficult to deal with the demands of her parent's job, and she had begun to resent the amount of time that the job required of them. She also hated the fact that she had to move a lot, going from one place to another on what in archaeology circles is known as 'The Circuit'.

Darcy felt the dull ache again in her chest. It was becoming a more and more common event and from nowhere. She wasn't prepared for the intensity of it. Breathing was suddenly hard. Her eyes stung. She blinked hard, and little trails of wetness made their way down her cheeks. Darcy had felt unwell for several weeks now, but she couldn't put her finger on the cause. Now, though, she had a moment of clarity. All this time, Darcy had thought her sickness was physical, a cold or something. Now she changed her mind. She was upset by the move and being forced to leave behind yet more friends. Friends were not a commodity Darcy had large amounts of in her life. Leaving Birmingham this time was so hard.

She breathed deeply. Suck in, blow out. The ache subsided. The 'dig' in the Midlands had finished.

That's that.

Darcy pushed a change of thought into her mind.

I'm on holiday.

She was pleased to get her parents all to herself again for a short while.

The ache is back.

After the holiday, she would start a new school when her parents took on their next job.

Breathe.

She rubbed at her chest.

For the next two weeks, I will have their undivided attention.

Darcy consoled herself with that as she finished the chapter of the book she was reading and lifted her head to look at nothing in particular out of the window.

What does it matter if I have to visit every ancient monument in the county, she thought. *I'm going to enjoy this.*

Darcy pushed her long red curls back over her shoulders and continued to stare out of the window. Tall and thin, no matter how much she might dislike the fact, there was no mistaking that she was a mixture of her parent's genetics. Her mother's eyes, her father's hair, and a bit of ingenuity, guts and stubbornness from them both.

Like a snail, the traffic began to make a slow procession down the road.

'Thank goodness!' said Pippa, 'we're moving.'

'Look at that sign,' said Tom. 'Services in half a mile, shall we stop for something to eat?'

His enthusiasm had Darcy and Pippa craning their necks to read it.

'Please Dad,' said Darcy, 'If I have to sit in the back of this car any longer, I'm going to melt.'

'That settles it,' said Tom. 'Her ladyship has spoken, and we must obey.'

Darcy saw that her father's eyes had mischief behind them. She turned her most indignant look on him. It failed miserably. Realising it, she settled for enjoying his 'dad joke'.

They pulled into a parking space, Darcy felt a warm, soft nuzzle on the side of her face. Willoughby, one of the dogs, had gotten up from where he was lying in the hope of sometime soon being able to relieve himself.

'Mum, I'm just taking the dogs for some exercise,' said Darcy.

'OK,' said Pippa. 'We'll go and order the food.'

If there's one thing Darcy is absolutely sure of never losing, it's the affection of her dogs.

'Good dogs, come on.'

She got out of the car and studied her surroundings. About a hundred yards away was a smallish copse of trees with plenty of shade and easily accessed. Darcy slipped collars over the heads of Marianne and Willoughby.

'Come on guy's, I've found us somewhere to walk.'

They headed into the coolness of the trees. The contrast from the stuffiness of the car was refreshing, Darcy began to feel more like herself.

Marianne barked. She was startled by something, Darcy walked over to her.

'What have you seen, girl?'

She ruffled the soft tufts of smooth hair on the dog's head, and Marianne snuffled at the ground.

'What's that?'

Just visible between a couple of trees stood a man. Darcy shivered; she felt a trickle of sweat run between her shoulder blades. There was something unusual about the stranger. His clothes were too big for his wiry frame, but it wasn't his clothes. He was average height; it wasn't his height either. It was his face, it shone. Darcy looked more closely. Even though there wasn't much light under the trees, she could see he glowed. A glowing mist surrounded him. He looked at her and smiled. Darcy felt in that moment there was nothing in the world that could hurt her, she was completely safe. Their eyes locked for a few seconds, and then, as quickly as he had appeared, he was gone.

Darcy looked everywhere, but the man had disappeared without a trace. It was as though he had never been there.

'Weird.' she said.

'Darcy! Where are you?'

It was Pippa. Jerked away from her thoughts, Darcy called back.

'Over here.'

Pippa turned to see her daughter emerging from the trees.

'There you are,' she said, 'the foods arrived, and we were getting worried. Are you alright?'

'I'm fine, Mum, Honest.'

Darcy really felt anything but fine. She was still thinking about the man in the woods. Deciding not to mention him yet, she let the dog's back into the car and followed her mother into the restaurant.

After a meal, the travellers made their way back to the car, very much to the excitement of Marianne and Willoughby.

Pippa drove this time and turned the car to re-join the motorway.

'Look.' she said, 'the traffic's really moving now, it won't be long, and we'll be there.'

Half an hour later, they were leaving the motorway.

'What do they call this place?' asked Darcy.

'Bodmin Moor,' said Tom. 'Look over there, it's the Hurlers.'

Darcy looked out. On the moor were several large upright stones. They reached out of the earth like stubby fingers straining to touch the sky. The stillness of the countryside and the colour of the stones gave the whole place a dark, secret feeling. Although Darcy had seen lots of ancient sites before, this one affected her in a way none of the others had. She started shivering. It was ridiculous on such a warm day. The feeling started in her arms and spread quickly to her legs. Darcy felt as if invisible icy fingers were moving up her body towards the centre, freezing as they moved. She was scared, but she couldn't speak.

Suddenly, she saw him again.

The cold Darcy experienced seconds before was gone. The man stepped out from behind one of the stones and looked right at her as the car moved past. Darcy stole a quick glance at her parents. They hadn't been affected by any shivering. Neither did they seem to notice the man standing amongst the stones.

Maybe they can't see him.

As this entered her head, she realised how ridiculous it was.

As the car moved on, Darcy looked back to where the man had been standing, but he was gone. She looked out of all the windows in turn, but there was no sign of him. Once again, he had vanished.

As they travelled closer to Bude, Darcy was still thinking about the man. What had he been doing at the service station? And then, how had he got to the moor at the same time as she did in a car? Why did he keep vanishing? Stranger even than all these questions was the fact that he gave her the feeling that he knew her?

Right now, Darcy had no answers. She just had an inescapable, frightening feeling of being watched, and it wouldn't go away.

'Look,' said Tom, 'Bude.'

The narrow road had opened out, and they were high on the side of a hill. Below was a small town. Darcy thought it looked as perfect as a picture postcard; thatched cottages along small winding streets and fishing boats tilted sideways, lying on the sand, waiting for the next tide to come.

They drove inland again, ten more minutes, and they pulled up by a sign on the side of the road it read,

'Welcome to High Bude Caravan Park.'

'We're here.' Pippa said.

Darcy couldn't see anything to be excited about. In front of them was a large field, busting at the seams with caravans of all shapes and sizes. There were hundreds of them, and hundreds of people in and around them, children playing, adult's talking and a lot of shouting.

'Noisy,' said Darcy.

They pulled up alongside a particularly scruffy caravan. Darcy's heart sank, her face followed. She had stayed at lots of different caravan sites over the years. Archaeology was not a high-paying job and caravan sites were cheap to stay in and everywhere. This one though was by far the busiest she had ever been to. Willoughby and Marianne wagged their tails excitedly.

'See,' said Tom.

He looked at Darcy's sulking face. He made his copy hers.

'They're glad to be here.'

Darcy gave him a fake smile and got out of the car.

The caravan was very scruffy. Dark orange streaks of rust oozed from all its joints. It may have once been white, but now everything had aged to a dull yellow cream. As Tom unlocked and opened the door, Darcy's disappointment grew. The inside living area was as aged as the outside. The mismatched furniture and the musty smell reminded Darcy of an old house that had been locked up, neglected and forgotten for years. Her imagination wandered. Darcy shook her head.

'No, stop it.'

'What was that?' said Tom.

Focussed again on the misery of his daughter's face.

'Nothing, Dad. Just nothing.'

Darcy moved through the caravan and found her space. It was not much bigger than a cupboard. A narrow window, through which the muted afternoon light was playing dancing patterns over the walls, was the only light source apart from a bare light bulb hanging from a cord above her head. She slumped down on the narrow bed and closed the door.

Tom and Pippa busied themselves, making the van more comfortable and unpacking their limited belongings. An hour or so had passed, and dusk was approaching. Darcy emerged from her room.

'I'm going to look around outside,' she said. 'I'll take the dogs with me.'

Stepping out of the van, the first thing Darcy noticed was that the day had cooled down. There was a pleasant breeze now, it ruffled her hair, she unexpectedly shivered. Marianne and Willoughby scampered around as they made their way through the maze of other caravans towards a narrow dirt track. Darcy's thoughts soon wandered to the stranger who had been following her all day.

Who was he?

He was like no one she had ever met before.

Did just staring at each other actually count as a meeting? Why didn't he say something?

She couldn't answer any of her questions.

It felt like he wanted to tell me something. What? I don't know.

'Hello,' he said. 'I've been waiting for you.'

Darcy's questioning stopped sharply. The man had a voice that reminded her of smooth, warm chocolate. She stopped walking and found herself looking up into his familiar face. He looked at her and smiled. The smile was friendly, and despite her wariness, Darcy couldn't help but smile back.

'I was just thinking,' she said.

'I know.' he said.

'How can you know?' she said, 'you can't just know things like that.'

'I know many things,' he continued. 'I know your parents drive you crazy. That your friends are few and that's how you like to keep things. Except for your dogs, of course, your biggest fans.'

He smiled down at Willoughby, who was nuzzling at his hand expectantly. Confused, the dog sniffed and moved away.

'I know that you have no idea who I am,' he said. 'For the moment, that is as it should be. I will tell you this though. Before too long, things are going to change for you. Events will be beyond your control or mine. Be prepared. I don't think you will recognise yourself much longer.'

Darcy laughed. She was very down to earth, not the kind of person unexpected things happened to.

'Why do you laugh?' he said.

'You must have me mixed up with my mother. She's the one who believes in all that mystical stuff. Me, I only know what I can see, what's real.'

'If that is true,' he said, 'how are you going to explain this?'

He vanished.

Darcy swayed. Her stomach lurched and nausea flooded her chest. She scanned one direction, then another.

Where had he gone? Did he run away? No. I would have seen it.

There was no sign of him, Darcy couldn't work out what had happened. She was more confused than ever.

Rounding up Marianne and Willoughby as quickly as she could, Darcy ran, dragging them behind her back to the caravan. She flung open the door and jumped inside. She had never been so pleased to see her mum and dad before. The vein on Darcy's temple, an exact replica of her fathers, pulsed. Her breath was quick and shallow. She rubbed at her forehead, squinting.

If this is what Cornish people are like, I'm never leaving the caravan again.

CHAPTER TWO

TREDINNICK'S EMPORIUM

The next day was as bright and sunny as the last. Darcy woke early to the noise of the caravan park. It was an unwanted alarm clock. Tom and Pippa were still sleeping. She could hear her Father's snores coming from another room in the van. She looked at her watch by the bed, 5.30am. Sitting up, she looked out the window. There were already people about, cooking, washing, just sitting around talking. Excitement was in the air. The eclipse was due to take place tomorrow, there had been lots of talk of what it was going to be like. From what she had been told, at some time in the morning, the sky would go dark for about two minutes, like at night. The moon would be precisely between the earth and the sun, blocking it out until all that would be seen is the fire ring around the perimeter of the moon.

Darcy was looking forward to watching it. Tom and Pippa had talked about going to Tintagel. Tintagel was a small town with a ruined castle that sat precariously on an outcrop of rock above the sea.

'It had been the seat of the ancient kings of Cornwall.'

Tom had told her this a couple of days before, and it was also where he thought he might get some work in the next year as a consultant archaeologist on an excavation. Darcy was sure that was the real reason why they had come to Cornwall in the first place. Tom had tried to make out that Cornwall was a fascinating place and a holiday there would be fun, especially with the eclipse happening, but she knew there was more to this holiday for her parents than just having fun.

Darcy watched as more people emerge from their vans to start the day. She got up, showered and changed. Tying her hair back and pulling it through just above the adjuster strap of her baseball cap. As quietly as she could, she made breakfast, trying not to wake Tom and Pippa. She hoped that if she just kept busy, she might not have to overthink what had happened yesterday, about the cold and him.

Cooking sounds and the smell of eggs and bacon wafting across the van towards their room woke Tom and Pippa from their sleep.

'That smells good,' said Pippa as she walked out of her room.

Darcy crossed to the table carrying two plates of food.

'I thought I'd surprise you on our first morning,' she said.

'Uh oh,' said Tom, his head appearing around the door, 'she's either done something terrible, and is trying to soften the blow, or she wants something, and is trying to butter us up.'

'Neither! I'm just nice,' said Darcy as she handed them both a plate of food, 'it's not like we get a lot of opportunities to do this sort of thing. What with your work and everything? I want today to be special, so let's just start with a quiet breakfast, and while we're eating, we can decide what we're going to do today.'

'Ah-ha,' said Tom 'the ulterior motive, better do what we're told.'

So, they ate. Halfway through a mouthful, Tom asked,

'OK, what's the plan for today then? Any suggestions?'

'I think we should go into town,' said Pippa 'I want to be nosey, and we need more supplies if we're going to eat like this every morning.'

Darcy agreed that town would be a good idea and keeping her parents there would mean that they would be miles away from anything remotely archaeological, or at least, that's what she hoped.

After breakfast, Darcy helped her parents clear away the dishes. They planned to leave for Bude later that morning, so after finishing her chores, Darcy went back to the book she was reading. In many ways, she was not your usual almost fourteen-year-old; she preferred reading to television, her own company or that of the dogs, to being surrounded by lots of people, and truth and fact, to imagination and invention. Pippa often told her that she spent too much time alone, or absorbed in a book, that she should get out more and spend some time with people her own age, but Darcy chose to ignore her, she liked being alone, and nothing was going to change that about her.

At about half-past nine, Pippa asked.

'Darcy, are you planning on taking the dogs for a walk today, or are you just going to let them whine?'

Darcy shivered.

'I don't want to,' she said.

Pippa looked at her, narrowing her eyes as she did so.

'Well, if you won't take them,' she said, 'I'll have to.'

Pippa put the collars on the dogs and stepped out of the van. Darcy felt guilt sweep over her like a wave. It wasn't Willoughby and Marianne's fault that she didn't want to leave the caravan, but she couldn't bring herself to go outside.

What if he found her again? He seemed to know where she would be even before she had decided where she was going. She knew that the fear she was feeling was completely illogical; he had never tried to harm her, but there was a strangeness about him that Darcy could not understand and until she could work out precisely what it was, he wanted with her. She was only planning to be in places where she was sure he wouldn't be.

Tom appeared from the direction of the bathroom.

'Where's your Mother gone to?'

'Out with the dogs.'

'What? You let her walk them?'

'Yes, for today, I just fancied a change. After all, isn't that what you're supposed to do on holiday?' Darcy gave her father a very narrow look. Tom knew exactly what she meant by it, but that wasn't what concerned him. She had never neglected the dogs before. He decided he would have to keep a close eye on her and see if he could figure out what was wrong.

Ten minutes later, Pippa, Marianne and Willoughby returned to the van.

'Good,' said Tom, 'are we ready?'

'Yep.' said Pippa, 'Ready when you are.'

'Mum, did you meet anyone on your walk?'

'Only campers.'

Darcy felt relief sweep over her. No sign of the stranger, she grabbed her ruck-sack and prepared to leave, maybe today would be just a typical uneventful day, without any surprises. That's what she hoped, anyway.

The drive down to Bude was very pretty. Quaint little seaside cottages, rolling hills with small farms scattered here and there gave way to dark steep-sided valley's, the sun unable to penetrate their cavernous expanses. Darcy enjoyed looking out at the passing countryside. Now and then she would check all the windows of the car to make sure he wasn't by the roadside or anywhere else for that matter, but the journey passed smoothly, with no interruptions.

When they arrived in Bude it was packed with people, Tom had to drive for half an hour in search of a parking space. In the end, they left the car and walked to the town centre. No one minded. The weather was wonderfully hot, and the walk was invigorating. Strolling down the steep, sloping high street was like stepping into another time altogether, old shops selling homemade sweets, and the usual buckets, spades and blow-up lilos associated with an English seaside town in the middle of summer holiday fever. Everywhere she looked, Darcy could see children and adults just enjoying themselves. It reminded her of a picture postcard and seemed difficult to believe that it could exist outside of it. The homes and shops that immediately bordered the narrow pavement were the colours of a box of crayons. Reds, blues, indigos, from pavement to rooftop, all butting up against each other. Wonderful smells of candy mixed with baked goods and then fish and chips made your senses almost want to explode. The riotous mixture of colours and smells was enhanced by the addition of hanging baskets containing summer plants that spilt out over the sides and trailed onto the heads of the shoppers as they ducked underneath to pass.

'Hi! Tom! Tom Bennet!' The voice came from fifty yards behind them and belonged to a man.

'I don't believe it.' Darcy said under her breath.

She had never met this man before, but there were sure telltale signs she had come to recognise as a dead giveaway for an archaeologist. Things like the well-worn trowel handle that just happened to be sticking out of his back pocket, the weather-beaten sun hat that looked like it was coming to the end of its usefulness, and the tan lines halfway up his shins from wearing socks with boots all summer.

Tom turned on his heels to see who was calling him. A broad smile crept over his suntanned face.

'Hi, David,' he called back, 'fancy seeing you here. Darcy, Pippa, this is David Williams, he's in charge of the excavations at Tintagel.'

'Great.' said Darcy.

Pippa heard and gave her a warning look.

'I was hoping I'd bump into you,' said David 'I wanted to discuss some work before we go over the site tomorrow.'

'Well, if you two are going to discuss work,' said Pippa, 'Darcy and I are going to leave you, we have some serious shopping to do.'

Pippa led Darcy off, and together they headed further down the high street.

'Thanks, Mum,' said Darcy, 'I don't think I could take a whole morning of Dad talking shop.'

'That's ok love,' said Pippa, 'sometimes there are more things in life than archaeology, and right now it's shopping.'

With a huge grin at her mother, Darcy grabbed her hand, and they continued off down the high street, joined arms swinging between them.

A short walk later, they found themselves outside a shop. It had a large shiny bottle-green sign that stretched from one side of the shop front to the other. Written in a bright gold lettering were the words 'Tredinnick's Emporium'. The sign sparkled in the sunshine and made up for the rest of the shop front which, unlike all the other shops in the high street, was rather drab and faded. The windows were impossible to see through. A thousand years of grime appeared to have accumulated unabated, to such an extent that Darcy and Pippa were unsure if they were windows at all. The invitation on the sign to 'step inside' seemed to draw them in with irresistible force and was too strong for Pippa and Darcy to ignore. They were being propelled, and although neither of them discussed going into the shop, before they realised what they were doing, they were already inside looking around at the items on sale.

Tredinnick's Emporium was no ordinary shop. The air was almost moist and hung with a musty smell that made Darcy's sinus twitch and tingle. Many of the items on sale she had never seen before, bottles containing dried animal parts, herbs and spices with names like 'Cuckoo Grass' and 'Codswallop Weed'.

'I wonder what that's for?' Darcy said as she picked up the latter.

'Fer makin' folk talk absolute rubbish,' said a voice from behind her. 'Very useful if 'ee find 'eeself bored silly by some good-fer-nothin' know-it-all. Jus' slip some into their tea, and sure enough, they'll start talking gibberish almost straigh' away. They soon disappear when they get fed up with 'ee fallin' about laughin' at 'em.'

Darcy carefully placed the bottle of Codswallop Weed back on the shelf and turned to see a small, plump, jolly faced Cornish woman behind her. She was as wide as she was tall and wearing a long dress woven out of something that resembled green gardening twine. Tied around her waist was a pure white apron. So white, that it seemed to glow, giving the impression that it had a power source of its own. The woman's face was reddened and weather-beaten, and her hair, silvery-grey, was piled high on her head in a lopsided bun. Darcy stared at her. But as hard as she tried, she could not work out what age this woman could be.

'Don't look so worried, dearie,' the woman said, 'I won't harm 'ee, I was wonderin' whether there be anythin' I can help 'ee with?'

'My Mother and I,' Darcy pointed a finger towards where Pippa was standing at the other side of the shop, looking through a box of what appeared to be scissors with one half missing. 'Well, we were just wondering if you do camping supplies?'

'Oh yes dearie,' said the women, she shifted her weight awkwardly from one leg to the other and back again, 'we 'ave all kinds of stuff to make a camp a bit easier fer 'ee, self ignitin' wood fer the fire, no need fer matches, even light's in the rain. Or maybe 'ee could do with some self cleanin' cauldron's, clean 'emselves right up they do, no need fer scrubin' 'em out.'

Completely flummoxed, Darcy was just about to turn and leave the shop when Pippa appeared beside her.

'Are you alright, love? You look a bit pale,' said Pippa.

She turned to address the woman.

'We were just passing, and the shop looked so interesting, we just had to come in and have a look around.'

'Tis' a wonder 'ee found us' said the woman 'not all of your sort can 'ee know's.'

'Our sort?' said Pippa.

' 'ee know's' the woman said, 'visitors, 'oliday folk.'

'Oh!' said Pippa, 'we were just looking for some supplies for our camping holiday, but you don't seem to stock what we need, so we'll be going now, but thank you for letting us look around at your lovely things.'

Darcy stifled a giggle at her Mother's attempt to leave the shop quickly without appearing rude.

'Oh, that's alrigh' me dear,' said the woman, 'come back and see us any time 'ee likes, we always likes visitors do we.'

Pippa and Darcy left. As she passed a counter, an all too familiar face appeared from behind it. It was the face that had haunted Darcy since she had come to Cornwall, and one that she had hoped she would not see again. The man stood so still. Only his beard twitched. He looked at her. Darcy stared back, unable to look away.

'Hello again,' he said.

Darcy only managed a feeble 'Hi' in reply.

'I'm glad you found this place; you're probably going to need some things from here before too long.'

Darcy laughed.

'You can't be serious, Codswallop Weed and half a pair of scissors? What use could I possibly have for them? Anyway, who's ever heard of such ridiculous things?'

'Oh, you'd be surprised what a useful thing a scissor is, especially when you're faced with a vicious Caucasus Buzzard.'

'Darcy!' Pippa called from the door 'who are you talking to?'

'I was...'

Darcy gestured towards the man, but he was no longer there. In fact, like every other time, he had just disappeared. She shrugged.

'I'm coming,' she said.

They both hurried from the shop.

'Well,' said Pippa, 'that was a bit strange, I don't suppose we'll be going in there again! Let's go see if we can find a proper shop that sells things we would want to buy.'

With that, they set off in search of a reassuringly average supermarket.

They meandered down the street, occasionally stopping to look in a shop window. Darcy's mind was now not really on shopping at all. She walked next to her mother, not looking where she was going. A couple of times she stumbled into an oncoming shopper.

'Be careful,' said Pippa, 'I really don't know what's wrong with you today.'

Darcy just could not get her mind away from the shop. '

What had happened there? What had the strange man been talking about? Why would she need things from that shop?

She was making herself more and more agitated with every unanswered question, but try as she might, reasoning things through, the man had given no clues as to who he was, or what he wanted from her. She came to a difficult decision. It had now become apparent that no matter how hard she tried to avoid him, he could find her, seek her out when he wished. She decided that the time had come to find out exactly what it was he wanted. Darcy was determined that if there was something that she alone had to be involved in, she was not going to go into it without knowing precisely what it was she was getting into. He owed her an explanation, at least. She made up her mind to tackle him about it the minute he decided to show up again.

'Look.' said Pippa.

Pointing down towards the very bottom of the street.

'A nice, friendly supermarket. Let's go find some food to eat. I'm starving.'

They entered the store, and Darcy pulled her mind towards her mother and the task at hand. Lunch.

CHAPTER THREE

PIXIE-LED

Darcy slept uneasily that night. She could have blamed it on the nocturnal animals that scratched their way around the dark caravan site, but there were other things, mostly in her mind, that disturbed her. She dreamed, dark dreams, they left her exhausted and shivering with cold. No sooner would she be done with one, than Darcy would sink back into a fitful sleep again to be engulfed by another. She stood alone on the dark moorland. There were strange shadowy shapes that loomed up out of the dark before her. When she was close enough to touch them, she reached out her hand. They were so cold, she could feel the cold moving through her fingers and up her arms, reaching for her heart. She retracted her hand quickly, and the cold left her. Then a voice, she could not tell from which direction, but she knew it or thought she did. It was his voice, but it wasn't as she remembered it. This time it was stern, angry even, and it spoke with authority, an important voice, a commanding voice—commanding her.

'Don't touch them,' he said 'they are the scourge of the moor, this was once a beautiful place, now it is cold, a place of death, they have named it Donyarth, the black ridge, these stones mark his territory, they possess his evil, otherworldly and alien. They can take a life if they wish.'

'Who's evil?' asked Darcy. 'Whose territory?'

'Narcasta's,' he said.

As he said the name, he became visible from behind the nearest black stone. This was not the man she remembered meeting in the shop yesterday morning. Or the one standing at the roadside, or in the woods. He seemed larger, powerful. His clothes weren't the simple clothes he had worn then, now they were robe-like, dark; he looked impressive, important, and suddenly she was terrified and freezing. His eyes were not calm, they burned with an inner fire, and she knew at that moment he could see her thoughts. That frightened her more than anything. Darcy heard her weak voice ask a question. it was as if someone else was speaking.

'Who is Narcasta?'

'He is the poison that plagues this land,' he said, 'you are the one who can help me save it, save Dumnonia. This your destiny, your future and our existence lie intertwined, his evil is not confined only to this world. Once he has all there is to take here, he will take what is yours, a destroyer of worlds, the destroyer of your world too if he cannot be stopped.

Go to the shop in town Darcy, Tredinnick's, Jenna will give you what you need to bring.'

He reached out his hands to her, but there was a flash, then nothing but darkness.

Darcy shot up in bed. She was shivering and cold, yet her pyjamas were soggy with sweat. She shook all over, unable to stop the tears from coming.

'It's just the shock,' she told herself.

But her heart pounding in her chest gave away the fact that she was scared. She knew what she had experienced during the night had all been a dream, but it had seemed so real. Yet here she was in their caravan, everything quiet and normal. How odd that sounded now. A few days ago, she wouldn't have believed that anywhere her parents were, could be called normal. Now, she found the familiarity of them comforting. The dogs were asleep by her side, calm and settled, but she could not escape the great sense of danger that had descended on her.

Just then, sitting in her bed, she was overcome by an irresistible urge to go outside, Darcy had no idea why, but she could not ignore it. She looked over at her alarm clock; 4.30am. Out of her window she could see the first light had begun to creep up over the horizon. Darcy got up, dressed quickly and tiptoed out the door. Once outside, she had no notion of where to go. There was nobody around, and it still wasn't full light. Darcy kept thinking she saw things in the shadows, shapes and movements.

'Don't be so stupid,' she told herself, 'it's just shadows.'

But she still had that irrational sense of danger with her. It made her breath catch slightly in her throat.

Darcy was just about to begin a walk down towards the sea when she saw two specs of light moving towards her. They were quite a way off, and she thought they could possibly be car headlights until they shot up into the air like a couple of shooting stars and then hung there for a few moments before moving off once more. That was it. Her inquisitive nature got the better of her, and Darcy moved closer for a better look. The nearer she tried to get, the farther away they seemed to be. Darcy didn't know where she was going. She continued moving towards the lights, onward until she noticed that the actual light around her was growing dim. Darcy looked away from the lights for a moment. She was walking into a wood, the trees around the perimeter were so tightly planted that they formed a canopy that stretched entirely across a small grassy area. She looked back to where the lights had been, but they had disappeared, and it slowly dawned on her that she was, in fact, now completely lost.

Darcy tried to remember the direction that she had come from, but it was hopeless. She had been concentrating too intently on the little lights that she could not remember which direction she had been walking in. Just as she was deciding whether to panic, she heard a barely audible whisper behind her.

'She saw us then Nix. What do we do with 'er now then?'

'Nothin'.' said another quiet, high-pitched voice, 'jus' wait, she'll spot us soon as she gets 'er bearin's.'

Darcy turned around. There, standing on a large, disc-shaped fungi protruding from the trunk of a huge elm tree, were two very tiny, very strange-looking people. They were both about the size of one of her hands. One, a female, or so Darcy thought, was dressed in green and purple striped tights, a green tunic dress with short sleeves and a lilac conical hat with a daisy on the top, her hair was long and wavy, and of the lightest sandy colour, it could almost have been white. Growing out of her back were two tiny transparent butterfly wings so delicate that they looked like they were made of a very fine gossamer. Her skin was ashen, and a broad grin brightened her face. Darcy was pretty sure this must be the one she heard called Nix. The other little person was quite different. Darcy thought it must be a male. He was wearing tight-fitting breeches, tunic, cap and boots all were an earthy green colour. His skin was fair too, but his hair was flame red; it made Darcy's look dull in comparison. He had wings also, but they were the same colour as his clothing, and she nearly didn't see them. His expression was much more severe than his partners, and he gave the impression of being in charge.

Darcy stared down at the little people, and they stared back. No conversation passed between them until she couldn't stand it any longer.

'Are you Faeries?' she asked, hardly believing she could be asking such a question.

'Faeries?' the voice was surprisingly loud for such a small person. 'Faeries' the word stuck in his throat. There was a bright flash of green light. Now standing in front of her were two people, they weren't little any longer; now they were the same size as an adult man and woman.

'We're no more Faerie than ee' are, an' never wants to be insulted like that again.'

'Sorry,' said Darcy 'I didn't mean to offend you.'

'We're Pixies,' said Nix, 'Faeries are sworn enemies, that's why Hicca 'ere was so upset, but he's fine now, aren't 'ee Hicca?'

'Yeh, I think I've recovered.'

His green eyes were gentle. In fact, now that they were so much bigger, Darcy could see their expressions quite clearly, and there was a certain aura of mischievous happiness about them both.

'I don't believe this,' Darcy said as if to herself, 'not only am I completely lost, but I'm stood in the middle of a strange wood talking to two people that can't exist.'

'You've been Pixie-Led,' said Hicca.

'But fer an excellen' reason,' joined in Nix. 'An' we do exist, surely your own eyes can tell 'ee that. We sees 'ee and 'ee sees us, that's enough existin' fer anyone.'

'What's Pixie-Led?' Darcy asked.

'That's what we do,' replied Hicca. 'Leadin' big folk astray is a kinda Pixie pastime but likes we said, there's a good reason fer us leadin' 'ee here. The Keeper can't come to find 'ee any more, too risky now. Narcasta found out he's been crossin' over, got those horrible birds watchin' the gate, they tells him everythin'; who's comin', who's goin', no one's safe anymore.'

'Narcasta? I've heard that name before.' said Darcy 'When was it?'

She stood there for a moment, thinking; and then it came to her, a flashback so sharp that it made her shudder. She was standing by the stones again, cold and frightened. He spoke that name. The first time she heard it was from him. She remembered the feeling of freezing ice sliding down her spine, that's how she had felt when he said it, that's how she felt now.

'Are 'ee alright?' said a small voice beside her ear.

It was Nix, who along with Hicca had returned to their former size and were standing on the low branch of the elm tree.

'Yes, I'm OK. I just remembered something that's all, but it's nothing, just a bad dream.'

But how could it have been a dream? Dreams aren't supposed to spill over into real life, so maybe it wasn't a dream after all. Darcy recalled the feelings she had experienced the night before, how intense they had been, how real. The line between what she considered reality and fantasy was becoming blurred. She was struggling to make any sense of it all.

'Darcy.' Nix spoke again, 'We must be quick, our time on this side is short, we 'ave to go back before we're missed. 'Ee must come with us. 'Ee must come and speak to him again, he has things to tell 'ee, he has to tell 'ee what 'ee must do. 'Ee has to come to the castle, the gate at the castle, it's a gate into our world, he is there waiting for 'ee. 'Ee must follow us, we must cross through before the darkenin', after that the gate will be closed, maybe forever!'

'Hang on a second,' said Darcy 'slow down, what gate? And what on earth is the darkening?'

'We can't waste time explainin' everythin' now,' said Hicca, ' 'ee 'ave to come to the castle, Tintagel you calls it, that's where we 'ave to go.'

'Tintagel,' said Darcy.

'Aye.' Hicca replied, 'that's the place. We 'ave to be there afore the sky goes black, afore the sun leaves the world.'

Darcy laughed.

'The sun doesn't leave, it's just an eclipse. It only lasts a few minutes, then everything will be the same as before.'

'No!' said Nix 'If Narcasta has his way, nothin' will ever be the same.'

Darcy stood thinking for a few seconds, then she remembered something from the dream the night before. He had told her to go to the shop in the town, to speak to Jenna.

'She will give you what you need to bring,' he had said.

She told the Pixies this. They started hopping around on one foot then the other in a way that Darcy could only describe as a sort of mini-panic.

' 'Ee must go now.' said Hicca, 'Ee is runnin' out of time.'

Darcy looked down at the watch on her arm, 7.15am. She hadn't realised so much time had passed. Her parents would be waking up and wondering where she was.

'I must get back.' she said. 'I'll meet you at Tintagel before the eclipse, don't worry, I'll be there, I promise. Which way do I go?'

Nix pointed to a little break in the trees.

'Hurry.' she said.

And then along with Hicca transformed into two specks of green light again and sped off into the morning sky.

Darcy ran back to the caravan in only a few minutes. When she arrived, she was out of breath and very tired. She crept through the door, Tom and Pippa were still sleeping, only Marianne and Willoughby noticed her return. Hurriedly she showered and changed. When she entered the main room again, Pippa was cooking breakfast.

'Morning, would you like something to eat?'

'No thanks Mum, I'm just going to pop into town before we go to Tintagel. There's a bus that leaves in 15 minutes.' Darcy produced a timetable she had found with the tourist information left in the van by the park owners.

'I should be able to get there and back in plenty of time, so you don't have to worry, I'll be fine.'

'If you wait a few minutes,' said Pippa, 'I'll be able to come with you.'

'No need Mum, really, I can manage by myself, I won't be long.'

'OK, I can take the hint,' said Pippa, 'just be careful, and don't take too long.'

As Pippa was saying this, Darcy was already through the door and hurrying in the direction of the Bus Stop.

Luckily the bus was on time, and soon Darcy was on her way into Bude. She didn't take much notice of the scenery this time, her mind was on the events that had already taken place that day. Strange dreams in the night that left her confused and frightened and turned out to be more real than her reality now appeared to be. Then there was the meeting in the woods with the Pixies; she still couldn't believe that she was involved in such a ludicrous series of events. Two days ago, he had told her that her life was going to change so much that she wouldn't recognise herself. She had laughed at him then; now, she had no option but to admit to herself that he had been right.

The bus ride passed quickly enough, and she was soon standing looking down the high street where she had been shopping with her mother only the day before. Now she could not remember where to go. Yesterday the shop had just appeared beside them as they had been walking along. She hadn't taken any notice of its position in the street, and they had hurried away so quickly afterwards that she couldn't even remember any of the shops near it. As she walked along, Darcy became more and more frustrated and had just about made up her mind to give up entirely and head back to the bus stop when the shop appeared beside her. The bottle green sign sparkling in the morning sunshine, and even though it was only 8.30am, the 'open' sign was clearly visible on the door. Taking a deep breath, she turned the handle and stepped inside.

The shop was darker inside than she remembered. It took a few seconds for her eyes to adjust after being outside in the sunshine. When at last she could see clearly again, she recognised the same strange things on sale that she had found the day before. Still wondering what use there could be for such items, she made her way to the back of the shop. The counter was precisely where she remembered. On top of the counter surface was a small brass bell, Darcy could see no-one about, so she picked it up and rang it. Behind the counter was a narrow corridor, and it was from here that she could hear footsteps gradually getting louder and louder the nearer the person making the sound got. After what she thought was an unusually long time to walk from a back room, a familiar smiling face appeared. It was the same woman that had served her yesterday.

The woman smiled and said, 'can I help 'ee me dear?'

Darcy was pleased to find her as welcoming as she had been on their first meeting. Same clothes, and the same lopsided hairstyle. This was reassuring.

'Please, can I speak to Jenna, I was told I could find her here?'

As soon as the words left her mouth, Darcy wished she had never spoken them. The light in the shop disappeared entirely, it was totally black. She couldn't see anything except a strange blue mist that was coming from where the women had been standing. As the mist cleared, the light levels in the shop rose again. Standing where the woman had been someone very different. Darcy had to reach out to the counter and steady herself. The woman now standing before her was possibly in her early twenties, tall and willowy. She had a beautiful face with startling midnight eyes. Her hair was the colour of raven feathers and fell in long curls onto the shoulders of a robe which was velvet and matched her eyes in colour.

'Where's the lady gone who was just here?' asked Darcy, not really sure she wanted to know the answer.

'You asked to speak to Jenna, I am Jenna, the other body I live in is just a disguise for the visitors. A witch is not much liked whatever place or time she finds herself in. Ignorance, intolerance and fear exist in more worlds than you can imagine Darcy. My disguise keeps me safe and makes me invisible to most people, I find that very convenient.'

Darcy soon recovered herself enough to tell Jenna about the dream she'd had. Jenna listened without commenting until she had finished.

'So,' she said, 'It begins then. Narcasta is trying to control the gateway, if he manages to do it, he will be able to cross into this world. The Gatekeeper is holding him back, but without help, he will fail. That's where you come in, Darcy. You remember your dream ended with a flash?'

Darcy nodded.

'That was Narcasta, he's trying to stop you from getting through, he cut you off from the Gatekeeper. I have a catalyst potion that can seal the gateway. The Gatekeeper knows this, that's why you were sent to find me, but Narcasta knows it too Darcy, he will try to stop you from getting it to the Gatekeeper.'

'Hang on a minute,' said Darcy, 'if you have a potion for the Gatekeeper, why didn't you give it to him yesterday when he was here?'

'Darcy, the Gatekeeper cannot leave the gate. He was never here, or in any of the other places you have seen him.'

Jenna's dark eyes glinted, and her full mouth turned upwards at the corners.

'Did you ever wonder why you were the only one who noticed his presence? He has been talking to you by mind-twining, a method of telepathy only the most powerful wizards can use, but this way of communication is dangerous, while he talks to you, his attention can't be on the gateway, you must see the difficulties this causes.'

'Yes,' said Darcy 'I can see how that's risky.'

'Wait here,' said Jenna, 'I'll go and prepare what you must take through the gate.'

Before Darcy had time to reply Jenna was racing around the shop busily collecting items from the shelves.

Darcy had never seen anyone move so quickly and skilfully. It almost appeared as if Jenna was walking on air. Darcy looked down at her wristwatch.

'Oh, no! 9.10am, the bus leaves in five minutes, I have to be on it.' she shouted across the shop to Jenna.

'Don't worry,' Jenna called back, 'there are other ways to travel, you'll get back in plenty of time.'

Just as she finished saying this, she came to a stop behind the counter once more, except this time Jenna was holding a colourful, patchwork bag, bulging with the things she had collected inside it.

'We don't have the time to go through all these things now and explore their uses, Mawgan will have to explain them when you meet.'

'Mawgan?' Darcy was confused.

Jenna continued, 'the Gatekeeper Darcy, he has a name—Mawgan—but he is not referred to by it often, and only then by friends. You have come to help us, so you are now considered a friend.'

Darcy thought she should feel honoured by this, but she was still so stunned by everything that was happening, she found it impossible to show it.

'Come now, follow me.' said Jenna as she walked off down the small corridor behind the counter. Darcy slipped under the counter hatch and hurried after her.

The corridor went on for an absolute age, Darcy thought she must be on the other side of town by now when they came to a small door at the end of the corridor.

'Jenna, how far have we walked?' she asked.

Jenna looked at her with a reassuring smile, 'You must have realised by now Darcy, that things are not always as they seem, nor where they seem to be.' Turning the door handle, they stepped out into the grassy clearing where Darcy had met the Pixies earlier that morning. Standing in silence for a few moments, Darcy trying to work out in her head how what they had just done could be possible.

As if reading her mind, Jenna said, 'Sometimes Darcy, it is necessary to believe first and find explanations later. You must keep your mind focused at all times, never let your prejudices and what you think you already understand to be true cloud your judgements, always be open to new ideas and new possibilities. Now, you must return quickly to your parent's caravan, you know the way, don't you? They will be waiting for you, the time of the darkening is fast approaching, and you must leave for the castle soon.'

Handing Darcy the patchwork bag, Jenna kissed her on the forehead and stepped back through the door crying, 'hurry.' as she went. The door quickly shut behind her, and Jenna and the door were both gone, with no visible evidence of ever being there in the first place.

The door closing was the kick that seemed to prod Darcy back to life. She quickly stuffed the patchwork bag into her own ruck-sack, so she could avoid any awkward questions from her parents. Then as quickly as she could, she ran in the direction of the caravan park.

Darcy struggled back to the caravan. She had made the same journey earlier that morning, but this time it seemed to take much longer. Maybe because the bag she was carrying, although only small, was incredibly heavy. Darcy had tucked it safely into the bottom of her ruck-sack, hoping no-one would think that important enough to bother looking in, though, she had no real idea what was hidden in it. When at last she made it back, she almost wished that she hadn't bothered.

'Where on earth have you been?'

Pippa looked like a pot just about to boil over the side, all red-faced and blotchy.

'I was so worried. You said you wouldn't be long, you've been hours. Your father and I were just about to get in the car and search for you. Don't you ever do that to us again.'

She could see the tears of relief welling in her mother's eyes. Darcy wanted to say she was sorry, to reassure her she was fine, but she wasn't sure she was fine at all. In fact, at that moment, she thought that she was anything but fine, Darcy couldn't let her mother see this, she had to keep a clear head. Jenna had told her not to get side-tracked by things, and she was beginning to understand how important this was.

'Mum, I'm really sorry, I just totally lost track of time, I've been absolutely fine, and we've still got time to make it to Tintagel before the eclipse. Dad can even meet up with -what's-his-name? - That David Williams fellow and talk about his site. If we leave now, we'll make it easily.'

Pippa seemed calmed slightly by the explanation, and Darcy quietly congratulated herself on being able to defuse what could have become an ugly scene.

'Come on then,' said Tom 'Get your stuff, let's go.'

Tom talked animatedly during the thirty-minute journey, about the dig, how long it had been going on, what had been discovered about the site, and whether they would be offered any work on it. Pippa, driving this time, quietly concentrated on the road, not really listening, still worrying about Darcy's long absence that morning and noting, not for the first time, her unusual behaviour. Darcy was silent in the back of the car, her thoughts a long way from what was going on around her.

'This is it,' she thought. Everything she had been told to prepare for was about to begin. Jenna and the pixies had told her about a gate, the Gatekeepers gate. How would she find it? What would it look like? Then a thought popped into her head. She nearly kicked herself for not thinking of asking him before. Jenna had told her earlier that morning not to let her own prejudices cloud her judgement, she had to stop letting her feelings control her actions.

'Dad, have they found a gateway at the castle?' she asked.

'They've found quite a few doorways, Darcy,' Tom replied, 'it was a huge complex of buildings with lots of uses.'

'Yes, but have they found any main doorways?' said Darcy.

'What looks to be the main entranceway has been located, yes.' said Tom.

'Whereabouts?' asked Darcy.

Tom passed her a little tourist map of the castle.

'If you look at the key on the side of the map, it shows you where the main gateway is thought to be.'

Darcy studied the map, searching for a gate or door or anything gateway like.

'What do you mean,' she said, 'thought to be?'

'Darcy, you know as well as I do that Archaeology has never been an exact science,' said Tom. 'A lot of the remains of the walls and doorways at Tintagel have been robbed-out, the stone would have been taken and used to build another building or repair an existing one. Tintagel's inhabitants over the years of its occupation made many changes. When we don't have absolute evidence, we have to make an educated guess, by comparing what we know about similar sites with what we've already found and filling in the gaps.'

Darcy looked at the map in front of her; sure enough, there was an entrance marked, but she had no idea if it was the one she had to find.

I'll just have to hope for the best, she thought, realising that at this stage there was little else she could do. Time was slipping away. Jenna and the pixies had said that she must find the gateway and the

Gatekeeper by the time the eclipse happened. That was due to take place in just over an hour. Once they arrived at the castle, she would not have much time to find where it was, she only hoped they wouldn't be very much longer in getting there.

'This is it,' said Tom five minutes later, 'we're here. We have to walk from now on.'

'What do you mean, Dad? Where are we walking to?' asked Darcy.

'Down there, it takes about ten minutes.' said Tom, pointing. 'Tintagel is built directly onto a cliff, and there is no other way of accessing it.'

Darcy was out of the car in a flash.

'You're keen.' said Pippa, 'I've never known you eager to get to a site before.'

The tone of her voice told Darcy she was forgiven for the earlier argument. For some reason, that felt important to her right now.

'I'm eager to see the castle,' said Darcy, 'I've heard a lot about it, you know, all the legends about Merlin and Arthur and stuff, I don't really care about the dig, that's your thing, not mine.'

Darcy found she sounded like her usual self. Pippa gave her a look of frustration, the kind she always gave when Darcy showed indifference to archaeological matters, and then looked away.

Darcy walked quickly, clutching tightly the rucksack containing the items from Jenna's shop. Walking was tiring. The pathway was steep and uneven in places, but she rushed on as quickly as she could. Darcy came to a set of steep steps that seemed to go on for an eternity. Looking back, she could see her parents still lagging quite a way behind her. She waved to them. They returned her wave and motioned for her to go on. Darcy needed little encouragement, she began to climb the stairs as fast as she could manage, carrying the bag, after what seemed to her an absolute age, she reached the top, and there it was. Sparkling in the reflections from the sea below stood the most beautiful, ruined building. The ancient castle of Tintagel was old and decaying, and yet in the sunshine, with people filling its walls, it seemed very much alive and vibrant, clinging relentlessly to the cliffs it stood on. She looked a long time, unable to move, thinking about it all until a hand rested on her shoulder and brought her back to the present.

'Dad.' she said, startled for a moment.

'Who did you think it was?' asked Tom. 'You're so jumpy, I thought you were feeling better?'

He looked at her in a concerned parental way.

'Come with us, there's something you've got to see.'

Darcy followed her parents down another flight of steps until they came to a small outcrop of rock on the cliffside. There they found David Williams and a couple of students from Exeter University doing a survey of the area.

'Do you know what they're doing?' said Tom.

'Dad, I've seen you and Mum do this a thousand times.' Darcy said, exasperated. 'That machine is called a Resistivity Meter, it sends electricity into the ground which resists it, and the resistivity is recorded by the metre. Stone walls, banks and ditches, stuff like that have a strong resistance, damp soil and such has low resistance.'

Darcy smiled smugly. She may not particularly like archaeology, but she made sure she knew enough to hold her own when quizzed about it.

'An excellent and complete explanation, we'll make an archaeologist of you yet.'

It was David.

'Perhaps you could show us where we should be doing it. We don't seem to be finding much today.'

'What are you looking for?' asked Darcy.

'A gate.' said David.

Darcy drew in a sharp breath. This couldn't be a coincidence.

'We have some old writings,' he continued, 'about this part of the site that say there was another section of building down here, though most of it has been lost to the weather and the sea, we might be lucky enough to find something.'

At that moment, Tom happened to look up.

'Oh! Quick,' he said. 'Let's go to the top again, the eclipse is about to start.'

He pointed to the sun, just over one tiny part of it, the moon had begun to cast its shadow. Tom, Pippa and David climbed the steps once more, Darcy, however, was rooted to the spot. Panic was the only emotion now running through her body. Her parents were walking on, deep in conversation with David and not noticing that they were leaving her behind. Darcy was used to being forgotten when her parents were distracted by work; usually, it irritated her. Now she was almost grateful for it.

'What to do now?' she asked herself.

She was lost for ideas. Was this the gate she had been told to look for? If it wasn't, she had run out of time to search anywhere else, and if it was, where was it? The remains of the building, if there was one, were buried under hundreds of years of dirt. It was then she noticed two familiar lights heading towards her from the direction of the sea. They grew larger as the sky grew slightly darker until she recognised the faces of Nix and Hicca flying to meet her.

The sky was growing darker by the second, the moon now almost half obscured the sun, and it looked as if it was twilight, not 11.15am.

'Good, 'ee found it.' Hicca called. 'I knew 'ee would, 'ee looks clever, I knew 'ee could do it.'

'Don't get too excited Hicca, we still have to get 'er through yet, that's the 'ard bit.' Nix said, giving him a withering look.

'Yes, but get me through where?' said Darcy. 'There's nothing here. There's no gateway to step through.'

'Darcy, remember not everythin's as it appears to be.'

It was just as Nix was saying this, that the eclipse reached its totality. As the last rays of sunlight were taken, an unexpected thing happened. About three feet away from the cliffside, directly suspended above the rocks a hundred feet below, against which the sea had beaten relentlessly for thousands of years, appeared a doorway. It seemed to have a dim radiance of its own, not enough to make it appear lit, but a phosphorous light, like the stuff in glow sticks. It was shaped like a lancet window in an old church, but instead of glass, there was a roughly hewn door which was covered in circular designs. Some of the designs looked a bit like trees. The door stood ajar. Its surround was stone, and it appeared to have a solidity that defied its mystical, ghostlike appearance. Darcy could just see through. There seemed to be a room on the other side, but much more than that she couldn't tell.

'Time to go Darcy,' said Hicca. ' 'Ee must go now before time runs out.'

'I can't, I'll fall.' Darcy said on the verge of tears.

'Darcy, 'ee must believe, 'ee can do it.' Nix reassured, ' 'ee have been chosen, 'ee must have faith in your abilities, just like we do. I believe in 'ee Darcy, we believe in 'ee.'

It was with these words softly reaching into her ears, that Darcy closed her eyes, put out her hand, feeling, in front of her, bit down hard on her bottom lip and stepped off the cliff into the doorway.

CHAPTER FOUR

DUMNONIA

The sensation of falling turned her stomach inside out. It wasn't the usual feeling experienced by a sharp downward movement, like when you ride a roller-coaster. It was the sensation of falling backwards; she was travelling back. The whole time she was falling, which could only really have been a few seconds, she was out of time, in a state of limbo. Darcy was unable to open her eyes. The nightmare of the sharp rocks below the cliff face rushing up to meet her flashed through her mind. Then, in an instant, it was over. A strong hand grabbed at her and dragged her into a nearby bush, she narrowly missed standing on a couple of hedgehog's asleep underneath it, she then realised it hadn't been a room she had seen from the other side of the gate, it was a walled garden. He put his hand over her mouth.

'Don't speak, he is searching for us.'

It was Mawgan, precisely as she remembered him in her dream.

In the shadows, she could see a shape moving around the garden, searching. It had a long-hooded cloak, so large that it covered every part of the body. Nothing was visible under the cloak apart from shiny red eyes.

'Who is it?' she whispered.

He answered her in a voice that was a low growl. 'Narcasta. He knows we're here, come on, we must be quick. Where is the bag Jenna gave to you?'

Darcy opened her rucksack and carefully removed the patchwork bag, giving it to Mawgan. Narcasta sensed their movement and turned sharply in the direction of the bush. Mawgan didn't notice, he was busy searching through the contents of the bag until he found a Mother of Pearl bottle with a glass stopper. The bottle was shaped like a teardrop, Darcy could just make out a swirl of dark liquid moving around inside.

'I must cast the spell to close the gate.' Mawgan explained, but just as he was saying this, a flash; a bolt of electricity narrowly missed them, hitting the main trunk of the bush, splitting it in two and setting it alight. A boney hand grabbed at the collar of Darcy's t-shirt. She was almost choking. Struggling to free herself, she got out from underneath the bush, her hair singed, and her clothes burnt, she pricked her hands on the spikes of one of the hedgehogs as she struggled.

There was another flash, this time green, something she recognised. The hedgehogs became Nix and Hicca, human-sized and glowing with rage. They grabbed and pushed her clear of another bolt of electricity from Narcasta. She saw Mawgan; he was lying face down on a stone path just to the left of her, his right hand still holding the bottle full of the potion. Swooping low and slamming themselves into his body were two enormous birds, they looked wild and hawklike, their eyes were steely, and their talons tore at Mawgan's clothes, ripping into his flesh. She instinctively grabbed for Jenna's bag, pulling out a scissor, like the ones she had first seen on her visit to the shop. She ran at the birds, wielding it like a sword. She cut into the first one's neck. It screeched, a terrible sound that bounced off the stone walls of the garden. Black blood gushed from the open wound, drenching her, and it flew up and out of sight. The other bird was on her in an instant, thrashing with its beak and claws, pummelling her with its wings. It pinned her down on the path beneath its enormous weight. Darcy had only one chance to move, and she knew it. She must be quick and decisive. Holding the scissor handle tight in her hand, Darcy thrust upward, hitting the chest of the great bird. She heard a horrible sound and knew it was metal slicing into bone. The bird gave an almighty cry that filled the air; she thought it would never end. Its great chest heaved, struggling for air. Suffocating in its own blood, it staggered off her and collapsed, narrowly missing Mawgan, heaving its breaths as it went.

Darcy lay dazed, in pain and disorientated for a few seconds; she could see Mawgan's injured body next to her. Hicca calling for her to get up brought everything back into sharp focus. The two Pixies were engaging Narcasta in a fierce magical fight. There were flashes of green and white light and what looked like lightning bolts coming from the battle which ranged over most of the garden. Their attempt to keep Narcasta occupied was working. Darcy struggled up and knelt beside Mawgan. Gently shaking him, she called his name. His back was scratched, and his right leg was bleeding badly. He murmured something so softly that she could understand him. Darcy struggled and pushed him over until he was lying on his back, touching his poor, horribly bruised face, she attempted to bring him back awake. Mawgan's eyes fluttered and opened. He looked up at her, a sudden awareness flashed across his face as he realised the gravity of their situation, Mawgan got to his feet, he had found strength from somewhere; he grabbed Darcy's hand and pulled her towards the gate.

'The eclipse will be over in a few moments, I must perform the closing spell now, Darcy you must go back to your world, once the spell is complete you will not be able to use the gate again.'

Darcy made to jump through the gateway, but she was suddenly rooted to the spot. As they had been recovering, Darcy and

Mawgan hadn't noticed that Narcasta had overpowered Nix and Hicca with one massive bolt of electricity that sent them both crashing into one of the stone walls. They now lay unconscious on the ground. Darcy could feel an ice-like sensation moving up from the souls of her feet, up her legs and through her body. She stood, not moving. It was the same sensation Darcy had felt in her dream when she had touched the stones. The same feeling she had sitting in the back of her parent's car. Cold bony fingers closed around her neck. Darcy could feel them trying to squeeze the life from her body. A scream formed in her throat, but his grip on her was so tight she was unable to release it. A flash of light and then scorching heat; she felt herself lurch off the ground, she felt excruciating pain on her forehead, and then she didn't know anything more.

Darcy floated in a dream state, unable to focus on what was happening around her. She thought she could feel herself being moved, but the effort of waking up was too much, and she rolled out of consciousness again. Then she thought she saw hills and open fields, but whether Darcy actually saw or imagined them, she did not know.

Slowly and with a lot of pain, she opened her eyes. The sky above her was a brilliant blue, soft floaty clouds skimmed across it. She worked out from this that she must be lying on her back, outside, but her head still hurt so much, that thinking was difficult. A familiar, friendly face came into view.

'You look terrible.' She croaked; her throat was still really sore where Narcasta had tried to strangle her.

'Thank you,' said Mawgan peering down at her, 'you don't look so great yourself.'

The bruises on his face were different shades of purple, and she could see that his cuts oozed a yellow liquid. It had a peculiar smell and Darcy didn't like the look of it.

'You've been unconscious for two days Darcy. We had to carry you, but we can't go any further, Nix and Hicca need to return home.' Darcy slowly moved her head look at Nix, who was only a few feet away, bent over the body of Hicca who lay still, too still on the ground. 'Hicca is very sick, he sustained a massive injury to his head when Narcasta flung them into a wall. I don't think there is much hope of his recovery. I have done all that I can, they must return to The Vale of Secrets, perhaps there is some remedy that their own people can administer.'

'The Vale of Secrets, what is that?' said Darcy.

'Not what, Darcy, where? It is the home of the Pixie folk, no one but their kind knows where to find it. Nix must take Hicca before it is too late, and they must go alone.'

Darcy reached out a finger and rested it gently across the shoulders of Nix. The little pixie lifted her face for a moment, big tears were flowing out of her eyes and streaming down her little pink cheeks.

'We 'ave failed 'ee Darcy,' she sobbed. 'Look at my poor Hicca, he can't go on, we 'ave to leave 'ee; an' with 'ee bein' stuck 'ere an' all.'

Darcy gathered the pixie up in her hand.

'Now look Nix, you take Hicca home and make him better; you mustn't worry about me. I'll be fine.'

She put Nix back on the grass, where the pixie suddenly changed form into a tiny ball of green light. The light moved over the body of Hicca, lifted him into the air, and they were gone in an instant.

'What did she mean, stuck here?' said Darcy.

'How much do you remember?' Mawgan asked her.

'I remember trying to go back through the gate, and I remember Narcasta grabbing my neck in his hands. Then I don't remember any more.'

'Things did get a bit confusing after that.' said Mawgan. 'Narcasta got away from the pixies injuring Hicca in the process. I saw him come up behind you. He would have killed you, Darcy, if I hadn't intervened and thrown you clear of his lightening. I managed to overpower him. He crawled off somewhere. He's no good without help. When you killed his buzzards, he had no choice but to fight himself. Not something Narcasta likes to do. He much prefers getting others to do his work for him. Not much of a sorcerer, is he?'

'A sorcerer?' said Darcy. 'I didn't know he was a sorcerer.'

'He likes to think he is,' said Mawgan, 'he's descended from a line of powerful Dumnonians.'

Darcy sat on the grass lost in her thoughts, Mawgan knew that she needed a few minutes to collect herself, so he left her alone.

'Mawgan,' said Darcy, 'you didn't answer my question.'

Mawgan looked squarely at her, 'I was hoping I wouldn't have to answer it, but I can see that you need to know. Darcy the gateway is closed, permanently.'

She stared at him, a mixture of confusion and anger on her face.

'What does that mean?' She snapped, half knowing that she was going to hate his answer.

'It means that you can't go back, you have to stay here with us. There is no other way back into your world.'

'But my parents,' Darcy sobbed, 'my dogs, everybody I know; they will be looking for me, they'll be so worried.'

'I know,' Mawgan said.

Sympathy and sadness showed all over his face.

'I can't stay here,' said Darcy, 'there has to be another way. Please, Mawgan.'

Tears rolled down her cheeks freely now, and her shoulders shook.

'I had no choice. The gate had to be closed, or Narcasta would have gone through himself. I'm so sorry, and now is not the time to dwell on such things. You are still far from well; we must get you help. Narcasta will come after us once he has gathered his people, he will not let us get away with what has been done. We must leave here, find a safe place. I think I know somewhere, but we must leave now.'

Darcy struggled to her feet. She felt dizzy, and her head ached unbearably. Mawgan took her arm, but he was not doing so well himself. She could see his leg now. He had a bandage made out of some sort of plant wrapped around the wound, but couldn't bend it, and at best he could only hobble along.

'Mawgan,' Darcy spoke softly, 'those birds that attacked us, what were they?'

'They were the Caucuses Buzzards, I told you about when we spoke in the shop.' he said. 'They live with him up there.'

Mawgan turned and pointed in the direction of the sea. It was the first time she had really looked around, and it took away her breath. In Darcy's world, Tintagel was a ruin, an echo of a past age; but here it was young, whole and very much the fortress it was always intended to be. High crenelated walls rose from the cliff as if they had grown out of the very rock itself. Massive watchtowers loomed intimidatingly over the countryside so that whatever direction you looked from, your eyes were drawn to them.

Darcy stood looking for a long moment.

'If my Mum and Dad could see this now, they would have a fit.'

On saying this, though, she remembered that she might not be seeing her parents again, and she realised how much she missed them. Being away from her parents was not something Darcy had experienced before. She felt pain and weight in her chest. She was becoming used to that sensation; it was how she experienced loss and fear. The pain made her unable to speak. She sunk to her knees again, hunched over with her head between them. Mawgan knelt beside her, unable to offer any comfort. Eventually, Darcy recovered enough for them to continue. They walked on in silence, the girl and the wizard, together and yet very much alone.

They headed inland down a yew tree lined trackway, as hours slipped by they walked on. The road was completely deserted. Darcy noticed a change in the landscape from an open coast to flat fields.

'Where are we?' she said.

'Almost there,' said Mawgan, 'why don't we stop for a moment, have a rest.'

Darcy could see that he was struggling and in pain, but she didn't say anything. Although Darcy hadn't known him long, she had the feeling that Mawgan was not used to admitting any kind of weakness. She leaned back on an available hedge bordering the field they were passing. Everything that happened next happened very quickly. There was a crack, and someone yelled.

'Oi! Ge' orff.'

Darcy was lying flat on her back on top of someone large, bony and uncomfortable.

'Who are 'ee?' said a gruff voice 'an' wha' do 'ee think 'ees doin' fallin' on unsuspectin' folk who is jus' goin' abou' their business?'

'Hello, Kea.'

Mawgan leaned over the hedge, laughing at what was going on below him. Darcy had fallen clean through the hedge and landed on someone picking turnips. When she righted herself, she realised that this was not some old farmer. He was a boy, about 15 years old, not very tall, but stocky and muscular. Thick wavy hair framed his suntanned face, and he had bright, kind eyes. Kea wore a leather waistcoat over his scruffy shirt and stowed away his cutting knife in the front breast pocket as he looked Darcy up and down, assessing her.

'We are on our way to your home,' said Mawgan, 'I was hoping you and your parents would be kind enough to look after Darcy for a while until she feels better.'

'There's nothing wrong with me,' said Darcy. 'I'm absolutely fine, just a bump on my head, nothing I can't handle. Anyway, look at you, if anyone needs help, I'd say you do.'

'Darcy, I have someone I must see,' Mawgan said, 'he is the head of my wizard order, and I must go on my own, he would not take kindly to me bringing a stranger, even one as important to us as you. It will only be for a few day's then I will come for you. Mr and Mrs Willow are kind people, you will be well looked after.'

During Mawgan and Darcy's disagreement, Kea had been occupied. He was squinting, shading his eyes from the sun and watching a tiny black speck grow on the horizon. It was still too far away to make out what it was, but it appeared to be moving in their direction.

'Wha' do 'ee recon tha' is?' he asked, pointing towards it

Mawgan grabbed Kea's waistcoat.

'You have to leave now. Run. Run as fast as you can and don't look back.'

'Why?' said Darcy, 'what is it?'

Mawgan replied with just one word, but that word was enough to strike fear into all of them. 'Buzzards.'

Kea grabbed Darcy's hand.

'Come on,' he said.

'What about Mawgan?' she shouted back.

Mawgan was already making his escape into the trees, calling as he went.

'Go on. I'll be back for you.'

Kea and Darcy ran down the track road as fast as they could. Now and then they would steal a glance behind them, they couldn't help themselves. The speck was gaining on them, now no longer just a speck, it had become clearly visible as a flock of enormous birds.

'We 'ave to 'urry or we'll never make it to my 'ome before they catches us. I knows a shor' cut through them there trees,' Kea said pointing, 'tis a bi' rough goin' bu' it's the only chance we've got.'

They ran for the cover of the trees; underneath was overgrown with tall bracken that scratched at their legs and whipped their arms as they ploughed a way through with their hands. When they reached the other side, there was an open meadow covered from end to end in buttercups, daisies and cowslip. At any other time, Darcy would have thought it a beautiful place, but she had no time to stop and admire it. All she could think of right at that moment was how they would get across it without being caught.

'My 'ouse is jus' the other side in a little dell,' said Kea, 'well hidden. If we can ge' across, we'll be safe.'

A cry pierced the sky above them. To Darcy's horror, there were not just two birds this time, but at least twenty, maybe more. They didn't hang around to find out. Leaping forward, Kea and Darcy sprinted for the far side of the meadow. Although he was heavier built than Darcy, Kea was quicker on his feet and turned, pleading with her to run faster. He was horrified at what he saw. Not more than a metre or so behind her a huge bird, talons poised for the attack, was bearing down. It was not alone. On its back rode Barrowman. A dark wizard, he was well known for being ruthless with the enemies of his master. Kea picked up a stone lying on the ground by his feet. His aim was perfect, and he hit the bird's head, making it pull up sharply. It squawked, shaking its head.

'Come on, Darcy.'

She found she could run faster than she had thought was possible. The adrenaline pumping through her veins powered her on. They made it into the dell. At the bottom stood the straw-thatched cottage known as Trecath-en. Tripping along the cobbled path, they jumped over the small wooden garden gate and flew in through the front door.

'Wha' the 'ells goin' on?'

A booming voice came from the small kitchen. It was Mr Willow. He had just come home for some lunch and did not take well to having it interrupted by his son and a strange, wild-looking girl bursting in through the front door. He was a hulk of a man, massive, with huge muscular arms well used to hard manual labour. But before anyone could say any more, a loud gavel sounding voice came from outside.

'Willow. I know you're in there. Bring the girl out, and you'll be left in peace. Come on, Willow, I know you have her.'

'Barrowman,' Mr Willow said to himself.

He turned to Kea and Darcy 'I don't know what's been goin' on around here, but I'm not gonna be told who I can and cannot 'ave in me own house.'

He grabbed his shotgun and stepped up to the front door.

'Barrowman, you're no' getting' your 'ands on me an' mine today or any other day for tha' matter. Go on back to that stinking 'ole 'ee crawled out of and tell that snivelin' weasel Narcasta, if he's got anything to say to me, he should come 'ere himself and say it.'

Barrowman was strong, but he knew better than to anger this farmer, especially in his own home.

'You've been lucky today, Willow. I'll be back for the girl, she has an appointment to keep with my master, and he is not in the habit of being kept waiting.'

The beating of many wings hitting the air all at once, could be heard above the house. They slowly faded away until eventually, the sound had gone completely. They were alone. Peter Willow turned his attention then to Darcy and his son.

'Now someone betta tell me what on earths goin' on.' He said.

CHAPTER FIVE

TRECATH-EN

Trecath-en was a perfect little house. It had white-washed stone walls and a thick straw-thatched roof. There was always a smell of something yummy coming from the kitchen, which produced all kinds of comforting food. Including what had become Darcy's favourite, sticky toffee pudding with sweet yellow custard. The furniture was wooden, worn and comfortable. Darcy had been given her own room. It was decorated in cream wallpaper with little pink rosebuds splashed here and there. Her bed was warm and cosy, every night she would sink into the deep, soft, spongy mattress and immediately fall into a peaceful sleep. There was nothing extraordinary about the place, but it gave her a feeling of security. This was something that Darcy had never really experienced before. She was always moving from place to place, a few weeks here and there. The longest she had stayed anywhere had been a complete dig season, which amounted to a summer. Darcy was becoming very settled at Trecath-en, and she loved the feeling of it.

After Darcy had recounted her story at length to Peter, Gwen and Kea Willow on that first day (which they had listened to open-mouthed and wide-eyed, gasping in all the appropriate places), she had gone on to spend a week with them. The wound on her head was almost healed thanks to Gwen's knowledge of herbs and how they were used in healing. She felt healthy and restless. The stronger she became, the more her mind was drawn towards things far away from this cosy home.

Darcy thought of her parents. The pain of missing them was physical. The tightening across her chest didn't fade. She knew they would be beside themselves, frantic with worry for her. She also knew that they would be furious and disappointed, thinking she must have purposely run away with no reason or explanation. The thought that they might think badly of her made it worse. She tried to think of something else. She applied her mind to the mystery of Mawgan's whereabouts. Darcy hadn't seen or heard from him since the day they had parted company, him running into the trees not far from Kea's home. He had called back to her, promising to come back. He had promised, but there had been no sign or word of him since. She was worrying that leaving her at Trecath-en had just been an excuse to get himself away from being around her all the time and feeling responsible. She was not supposed to be here. If everything had gone to plan, she would have returned through the gate, and all would be back the way it should be.

Darcy sat looking out the little wood-framed window of her bedroom. It gave her a clear, uninterrupted view of the cobbled path leading out of the dell. She pulled up the sash and gulped in long breaths of the sweet, musty air. It had been an endless week, unable to venture out for fear of being caught by one of Narcasta's people. Or worse, attacked by the buzzards again. Darcy had spent a lot of time absentmindedly staring out of windows, not really knowing what she was hoping to see. At first, she had wondered why Narcasta had not tried to take her by again by force. Then once she had seen Peter Willow giving Kea a hunting lesson. His strength and physicality helped her conclude that he was not a man to get on the wrong side of a fact, she was sure, Narcasta knew too.

She turned from the window and looked again around the little bedroom, a cool breeze caught the hairs on the back of her neck, it was uncomfortably chilly, and she shivered involuntarily, turning back to the window again intending to shut it. The old yew and ash trees in the dell swayed in the breeze. She heard them creaking and groaning. It reminded her of the sound old people make trying to get out of chairs they have sat in too long. Darcy screwed up her eyes. Straining, she thought she could see something. She looked harder. Sure enough, she did see something. It was two people, just visible, making their way down the path. One was quite young. She could tell by the way he carried himself. His skin was dark, and his long hair fell in dreadlocks over his shoulders. His walk bizarrely was like floating. Darcy was reminded of the travelators at airports. She remembered that strange sensation of walking while the travelator was moving quickly. Darcy scrutinised him and promptly came to the conclusion that he was a bit too full of his own importance. It wasn't this stranger though that made her jump up in excitement. The other person was older, his hair and beard were straggly, and his clothes were scruffy with many days of travelling. Nevertheless, he still walked with determination and a very pronounced limp.

'Mawgan!'

Darcy called out of the window.

She was frowning a bit as she shouted his name. Mawgan looked up and waved, and Darcy's frown was instantly replaced by a broad smile that stretched across her worried face.

'It's good to see you, Darcy,' Mawgan called, 'you look well.'

'Yeah,' she shouted back 'you don't.'

Darcy looked disapprovingly at Mawgan's leg. He made a return gesture that brushed her concern off.

'It's nothing,' he said.

Darcy wasn't so easily convinced. While all this was taking place, the other wizard just looked up at the sky, distracted.

Darcy ran down the stairs into the small hallway.

'Kea! Kea! He's here! Mawgan's here!' she shouted.

Kea appeared from the kitchen. Darcy clicked her tongue.

'You're not eating again, are you?' she said, 'it's only been an hour since breakfast.'

'I-as-ungry,' said Kea.

Darcy couldn't make out what Kes was actually trying to say, as he continued to stuff what was left of the giant chicken sandwich he was holding into his mouth, a smile spreading across his face.

'wha-wa-you-sain?' Kea squeezed out between chews.

Darcy rolled her eyes towards the ceiling.

'I-said-Mawgan-is-here,' her voice slow and exaggerated.

Kea swallowed hard and ran towards the door.

'There's someone with him,' said Darcy.

'Who?' Kea stopped and turned to look at her.

'Well, how would I know?' said Darcy, 'I've never seen him before. I've only met seven people since I've been here, and he's not one of them.'

'What does he look like?' Kea asked. Now it was his turn to roll the eyes.

'He's tall, black and looks like he thinks he is really something,' she said.

The smile on Kea's face spread even wider at this news.

'Great,' was all he said as he hurried to pull open the heavy front door.

Mawgan, on closer inspection, looked worse than Darcy had first thought. The eye's that had been so clear and interesting were now bloodshot, and there were huge dark rings around them. His hair and beard were straggly and unwashed. Darcy also noticed that his face was covered in even more cuts and scratches than the last time she had set eyes on him. Had he been in another fight? Mawgan smiled as he hobbled in through the door. His injured leg was still a problem to him.

Darcy made the decision that now was not a good time to discuss with Mawgan just how bad he looked, or that she was furious at him for dumping her. She quickly deduced that he had not been having the best of times himself. In fact, she concluded that she had got the better time of the two. Darcy hugged him. Kea shot her a warning glance. Mawgan was startled. He stretched out his arms away from her as she clung to him. Slowly he relaxed until he was hugging Darcy right back. He smiled as he indicated at the wizard who had just appeared in the crowded doorway,

'This is ...'

'Glewas,' said Kea, patting the wizard firmly on the back.

Darcy took her first intentional look at this stranger. He was younger than she had first thought, only a few years older than herself. Glewas was exceptionally tall. Everything about him was immaculate, right down to his shiny black boots. Darcy, however, was not interested in what he was wearing. She had noticed something that was considerably more important to her at that moment. Glewas was handsome. Darcy was suddenly very much aware that she was wearing one of Gwen's old dresses and that she hadn't brushed her hair today.

Mawgan limped into the living room and slumped unceremoniously into one of the Willows' overstuffed chintzy chairs. He looked a picture of dejection, his 'there's nothing wrong with me' act obviously becoming too much for him to make believable anymore. Darcy followed behind him, unable to hide the look of concern on her face.

'Where have you been?' said Darcy. She knelt by his side. 'I thought you had forgotten about me.'

'I'm sorry you were left so long Darcy,' said Mawgan, 'but there has been a lot to do and not much time in which to do it. I have been to many places. It is better if you don't know the details, but I can tell you we are not without hope.'

'You're talking in riddles, Mawgan,' she said, 'what do you mean, 'not without hope'?'

By the time she had asked the question, Mawgan's eyes had rolled back, and sleep took hold of him.

While Darcy was with Mawgan in the living room, Kea had been talking with Glewas in the hallway. Darcy could hear their conversation now that Mawgan had passed out. She stole a look at them from where she was kneeling. Glewas and Kea really were as different as it was possible to be. Glewas' tall, dark looks made Kea look short and clumsy. Darcy could tell though that they knew and liked each other well. She strained to hear what they were saying.

'... where did she come from?' asked Glewas, his voice deeper than Darcy had expected.

'I dun' know, really,' said Kea, 'through some gate, Mawgan was lookin' after. She was helpin' him ee' knows.'

Glewas looked over to the chair where Mawgan was sleeping.

'He's been in a real state, I found him on the road coming back from a Wizengan Meet. But you mustn't say that I told you, the meetings are supposed to be secret, I could be in a real bother for even mentioning that there had been one recently.'

'Don't go frettin' eeself,' said Kea, 'I won't be tellin' no-one. Did he say what's to be done next?'

'I couldn't get much out of him,' said Glewas, 'he just kept on insisting that we got here as soon as we could, wouldn't even stop for any rest, just said he had to keep moving and that he mustn't get caught by any of Narcasta's lot.'

Mawgan stirred and mumbled something in his sleep.

'Imps—rotten Imps—need to stop the messages—must stop.'

Darcy didn't know what he was talking about, but Kea and Glewas had heard and became very interested.

'Has he said anything else?' Glewas asked Darcy.

He stared at her. It made her nervous. Mawgan started to speak again, Glewas and Kea came over to hear.

'Pixies—must tell—must find secret.'

But after that, his words became nonsense, and he was soon snoring heavily.

'Well?' said Glewas, looking at Darcy again.

'I—er—no—I mean—no. At least, I don't think so.'

Stumbling over her words, Darcy turned away, screwing up her face in frustration. Glewas didn't notice that he unnerved her. Kea, on the other hand, found the whole thing very amusing.

'What are you grinning about?' Glewas asked him.

'Oh, nothin'. What do ee' recon all that were abou' then?' said Kea.

'I'm not sure,' said Glewas, 'but I'm pretty certain I heard him say something about the Imps.'

Kea nodded.

'Yea, I heard that too,'

'What are Imps?'

Darcy had recovered herself enough to re-join the conversation.

'are ee' back with us then?' Kea smirked. Darcy felt the blood rush to her face but hoped that neither of them would see it.

'I think it's time we all had a chat and try to fill in some gaps,' said Glewas, 'maybe between us, we can come up with a complete picture?'

Darcy took this to mean that she was expected to re-tell her story. She was growing tired of doing this every time someone new came along.

Although it was summer, the day had been cold, and Gwen had lit the fire in the grate of the huge inglenook, it now bathed the room in a warm glow and threw dancing patterns onto the walls. Kea, Darcy and Glewas settled themselves on cushions in front of it. Darcy told her story as completely as she could, but there were still parts she didn't understand. Glewas listened to every word, nodding now and again as if she had confirmed some idea he had been playing with. After an hour, Kea's concentration was failing. He had heard this all before, and his eyelids felt like they were being weighed down with something heavy. The fire had a hypnotic effect, and Kea felt waves of sleep lapping over him. Just as he was drifting out of consciousness, a sharp prod made him sit bolt upright.

'Wha—wha—what's the matter?' he asked.

Kea rubbed at his eyes.

'I just wondered whether you had any idea what Mawgan was going on about the Imps for?' said Glewas.

He was unconcerned and unapologetic that he had made Kea jump in surprise.

'Dun know,' Kea said. 'But didn't he say somethin' 'bout messages?'

'Yes,' said Darcy. 'I heard that too, but what are Imps anyway?'

'Imps are rotten little blighters,' said Kea. 'They were brought 'ere by Narcasta. Usually, they live up in the north somewhere.'

'Doonland I think,' said Glewas.

'Yea, that sounds 'bout righ',' Kea continued. 'Well, he brough' 'em down 'ere to do a job fer him. 'Ee see, they're righ' small, a little bigger than the Pixies but not much. Anyway, they run his messages fer him, from all his spies, they're speedy and when they're travlin' 'ee can't see 'em, they're so fast they're invisible.'

'You forgot to mention that they are completely evil,' said Glewas.

'I were jus' gettin' to that bit,' said Kea.

He was annoyed that he had been interrupted yet again.

'Like he said, they're little blue scraps of evil. As payment fer doin' his work, Narcasta lets 'em hunt wherever they wants, 'undreds of 'em, altogether. If they catch 'ee they'll suck the lifeblood righ' out of 'ee like big blue mosquitoes.'

Kea screwed up his face for effect. Darcy felt a cold shiver move down her back.

'Have either of you ever,' she struggled to think about it.

'Well, have you ever been caught by them?'

'A stray one bit me on the leg once,' said Glewas. 'It took me an hour to persuade it to let go. The bite mark was there for weeks. You can still see it.'

He rolled up his trouser leg to show the scar off to full effect.

'They've got hundreds of little razor teeth, made a right mess, see.'

He pointed at and prodded the scar.

'How did you get it to let go?' said Darcy.

She wasn't sure that she really wanted to know the answer.

'My father once told me they hate fire,' said Glewas. 'They're terrified of it. Anyway, I set light to its tail. The thing let go of me pretty quick after that. It ran off into the wood with its back–side all alight, I could hear it for ages, squealing and swearing in that screechy Pictish voice they have.'

The three of them looked at each other for a second, then Darcy, hand over her mouth to stifle what was coming, laughed. The laugh was infectious. Kea chuckled, swallowed, then chuckled again, until he was unable to keep a lid on it any longer. Briefly glancing across at Glewas, Kea's head rolled back, and he emitted a huge belly laugh. Glewas, more amused by the efforts of the other two to contain themselves than the original reason for the laughter, let go of his haughtiness and laughed out loud.

'What's all this?' said a voice from behind them.

Turning around, they saw Mawgan peering down from his chair.

'How do you feel?' said Darcy.

'You should have woken me.'

Mawgan gave them all a stern look.

'There is much to discuss and prepare, but thank you, Darcy,' his face softened, 'I feel quite refreshed. Now what's all the commotion about?'

'You talk in your sleep, Mawgan,' said Glewas.

'What has that got to do with anything?' said Mawgan.

'Well,' continued Glewas, 'you mumbled something about the Imps, and we were just explaining what they are to Darcy here, she's never seen one.'

'I'm glad to see that you find the subject of Imps so funny, Glewas,' said Mawgan. The stern look returned to his face. 'I, on the other hand, find them repulsive and dangerous. Imps are leeches, and they will have to be stopped, but first, there are more immediate concerns. Kea, I wonder if your most excellent mother could be persuaded to provide a little refreshment? I feel quite hungry now that I've had some sleep. Besides which, I always find that food can clarify one's thinking, and it's clarity of mind that we will be most in need of today.'

Kea got up.

'I'll go an' see.'

He left the room in the direction of the kitchen. Darcy got up too and addressed a question at Mawgan.

'When you were talking about the Imps, while you were asleep, you said something about messages and that they must be stopped. What did you mean?'

'We must concentrate on one problem at a time Darcy,' said Mawgan. 'The Imps are a concern, but they are not my primary one. Come on, let's go and eat, there's a lot to discuss.'

Darcy hated it when people avoided giving her a straight answer. She had hoped since it was mostly his fault that she was now stuck here, that Mawgan would be more open with her, but just the opposite, he was cagier than ever.

The table was fit to collapse with the weight of all the food laid out on it. When Gwen Willow put a bit of food together, as she was often heard to call the process, there were no signs of a light snack on the horizon. You would consider yourself extremely lucky if you got away without being pressed into eating third or fourth helpings. Mawgan, Glewas and Darcy took their seats around the table. The three were overwhelmed at the amount of food they were expected to consume. Only Kea looked unphased by it all and got stuck in, piling his plate as high as he could, before stuffing large quantities of roasted chicken and potatoes into his mouth. Darcy thought he was going to choke, but everyone else was unconcerned, so she too joined in with the eating.

'So Mawgan,' said Darcy. 'what have you got to tell us then? You've hinted at things, but so far you haven't told us any more than we have already worked out for ourselves.'

She looked at him steadily. Mawgan sighed.

'Very well, you've been patient.'

'More than the patient,' said Kea. 'She's been a bloody saint if ee' asks me.'

'No one was asking you, Kea,' said Glewas.

He looked across at Mawgan and nodded.

'Darcy, do you remember, before I left you with Kea last week, I told you I needed to consult with the head of my clan?'

'Yes,' she said, 'I remember. Did you contact them then?'

'Yes,' said Mawgan. 'he was very troubled by your situation. So, we two together consulted an Oracle. He was convinced that there must be another way to get you home.'

'An' is there?' said Kea.

He resurfaced from his plate of food with half a chicken hanging from his mouth.

'Wait a minute,' said Darcy. 'What's an Oracle? I want to know more about that.'

'Not what Darcy, who,' said Glewas. 'An Oracle is the wisest, most knowledgeable wizard alive. He is the custodian of the collection of Dumnonia's recorded history.'

'So, he's a librarian?' said Darcy.

'In a way, yes,' said Glewas. 'Although it is a very honourable position and only the greatest of wizards get to be known as Oracle.'

'What's this got to do with me going home?' said Darcy. 'I presume that's where this is going?'

She looked again at Mawgan.

'You are frustratingly impatient sometimes, Darcy,' said Mawgan. He was smiling.

'The Oracle was able to find information of a time when crossing between our worlds was common, and gateways were everywhere and in use all the time. At a solar eclipse, the gateways are easy to find, as you experienced, but there is a way to reveal a gateway at other times too.'

'How?' said Kea.

'By use of a compass,' said Mawgan.

'A compass!' said Darcy. 'Let's go and get one. Mrs Willow!'

She called towards the kitchen. Gwen Willow stuck her head around the door.

'Would you or Mr Willow have a compass I could borrow?' said Darcy.

'Wa's a com—compass?' said Gwen.

Darcy screwed up her face, then let it fall back into its natural expression.

'Surely everyone knows what a compass is?'

She looked at the other faces around the table, and except for Mawgan, they all stared blankly back at her.

'Darcy,' said Mawgan.

His eyes were full.

'Yes,' she said, almost in a whisper.

Mawgan took her hand.

'There hasn't been compass in Dumnonia since before the time of Narcasta, and no one at this table remembers when that was.'

Darcy looked at her hand in Mawgan's large, craggy one. Right then, she felt small and alone, for all the supportive, concerned faces around her.

It was Kea that broke the silence.

'So, wha' now?' he said.

'Now we find a compass!' Mawgan said, patting Darcy's hand reassuringly.

Always the practical one, Glewas put his hand on Mawgan's shoulder.

'How are we going to do that? I've only read about compasses in books. I've never seen one, and I'm pretty sure Kea here wouldn't have a clue either.'

Kea, who had gone back to eating, was chewing enthusiastically and shook his head without looking up from his plate.

'Pixies!' said Mawgan. 'They'll know where to find a compass and how to use them. All we have to do is find the Pixies.'

'Mawgan,' said Darcy. 'No one knows where to find the Pixies, the Vale of Secrets can't be found, you told me that.'

'There is someone who may be able to help us,' said Mawgan.

Everyone's attention was now very much on him.

'Morwenna.'

'Who's Morwenna?' asked Darcy.

'She's a witch, Kea said. 'e shouldn't be encouraging any of us to be going near a witch. There are stories an' the like. It ain't natural what they do. Besides Mawgan, witches aren't known for being right friendly like?'

Mawgan looked across at Kea.

'I find that when you treat people with kindness Kea, they are more likely to respond with the same. Morwenna is sister to Jenna, Darcy. She will receive you. It's been a long while since she had news of her sister.'

Darcy's face brightened. She remembered the woman from the shop in Bude. She had liked Jenna. The thought of meeting her sister made home feel not quite so far off.

'How can Morwenna help us with finding the Pixies?' said Glewas.

'Morwenna is the only person alive to have seen the Vale and lived,' said Mawgan. 'If she is willing, I am hoping she can help us do the same.'

The group around the table continued to discuss many things, including how they could go about locating a usable compass. A few miles away in the village of Piddleton in the home of Morwenna Tredinnick, a meeting of a very different kind was taking place.

CHAPTER SIX

SECRETS AND PIXIES

Morwenna sipped her tea and sighed. The warm liquid was soothing, and she closed her eyes, rested her head gently on the back of her chair and put her feet up on the low table. She was tall and lean, her long dark hair fell loosely onto her shoulders, and contrasted with the deep red dress that reached to her ankles and tied at the waist with a thin gold belt. She was not obviously pretty, but there was something about her face, particularly her vibrant eyes, milky white skin and expressive mouth that held your attention.

Opening her eyes again, she looked about the room. Her possessions comforted her with their familiarity. The fire burning merrily in the grate and warmed her blood. A sudden noise from the direction of the front door brought her attention sharply into focus. She put down her mug of tea and stood up. The creaking noise she now heard was something entering the house without an invitation. Morwenna froze, listening for any sound that might tell her who this person or thing was. Leaning towards the fireplace, slowly so as not to make a sound, she picked up the knife from the mantlepiece. It had a small blade, the ebony handle glinted in the firelight, illuminating its carved surface. She used this knife to collect herbs and plants. She heard the creaking of a floorboard in the hallway, just outside the room. Her hand tightened on the knife handle, ready for whatever was coming.

'Good evening, Morwenna,' said a voice.

A thin bony hand, filthy, covered with tattoos and saggy with age, appeared on the doorframe. Slowly, the bent body of an ancient woman appeared in the doorway. She was withered and smelt of a mixture of mould and incense. It made Morwenna's nose twitch involuntarily. The old woman was dressed from head to toe in black. Her eyes were as dark and lifeless as her clothes, and they stared, dead, at Morwenna now.

'What do you want Tryfena?' said Morwenna.

She had moved her knife hand behind her back.

'I wanted to see if you were alone, I see now that you are,' Tryfena said.

Scanning the room for further occupants.

'The Master is interested to know if you have met with any strangers recently.'

'What possible reason would strangers have to seek me out?'

Morwenna scowled at her visitor.

'If you have seen what you came to see, please leave. I didn't invite you here, and I certainly don't want you to stay.'

'The Master will be very interested to hear about your lack of hospitality.'

Tryfena's voice was croaky.

Morwenna drew her breath in through clenched teeth.

'I don't care what he thinks, he's no master of mine. Now get out and tell your master to mind his own business.'

Morwenna walked out of the room, pushing past the old woman who was still holding onto the doorframe, almost knocking her over. When Morwenna reached the front door, she swung it wide and stood aside. She drummed her fingers against the doorframe, waiting for Tryfena to walk the length of the hallway and step through. After what seemed an age, the old woman finally made it. Morwenna slammed the door hard behind her. She had no intention of engaging in usual farewell exchanges with Tryfena. She breathed a little easier now the old witch was gone. Walking back into the living room, she sat and picked up her tea again, only then realising that she was still clutching the knife in her other hand.

The light outside Darcy's bedroom window was dying. The night was fast lowering its black velvet blanket over the world. It had been a long day. Their discussions had gone on for hours, but finally, the decision was made on what they should do next. Darcy was now in her room, gathering together the few possessions that had been given to her by Gwen and the rucksack with Jenna's patchwork bag. She still hadn't dared to look at its contents beyond what she had seen there the night Mawgan had closed the gateway. She was still afraid of what she might find. Jenna had said that she was a witch and try as Darcy might to ignore her own superstitions, this still frightened her a little, even though she liked Jenna. She didn't want to take any chances with the possessions of a witch, even one apparently as nice as her.

Looking about the room, Darcy's eyes were full. For a moment she thought she could hear her mother calling her from some other part of the house. Was that her dad she could hear laughing somewhere in another room? Darcy's cheeks were wet now. She sniffed and wiped at them with her hands. Darcy screwed up her face, cringing at the memories of how badly she thought she had treated her mum and dad. What did it matter what they wore or how they looked? It just didn't seem important anymore. Tears flowed down her cheeks again. This room was the closest she had felt to home the whole time she had been here in Dumnonia, and now she was about to leave that behind too.

'Darcy!'

Someone was calling her from the downstairs hallway.

'Darcy!'

Mawgan's voice was urgent.

'Are you ready to go?'

She looked around the room once more, closed the door behind her and descended the stairs. Mawgan, Kea and Glewas were waiting for her by the front door, dressed in heavy coats, hats and scarves. She quizzed Mawgan with a smile as she hit the last step.

'It's summer,' she laughed.

'That's as maybe,' he said, 'but we'll be travelling at night to avoid detection and summer nights in Dumnonia can be freezing even after the hottest of days.'

Gwen Willow entered the hallway carrying an old wool coat and well-worn hat, scarf and gloves. Darcy put them on. The coat was so big on her it brushed the floor.

'Well, it's the best I can do,' said Gwen. 'At least you'll be warm.'

She straightened Darcy's hat on her head and laid her hands on Darcy's shoulders for a moment before wiping away a stray tear on Darcy's chin. Gwen then turned to her son and grabbed him up into a huge bear hug. Kea screwed up his face.

'Time to go,' said Mawgan.

He laid a hand gently on Gwen's arm.

'We'll be safe,' he said. 'Nothing to worry yourself about.'

The four stepped out into the night.

'Mawgan was right,' Darcy said to herself. 'It's cold.'

She wrapped the coat tighter around herself. The dell was very dark. It was hard to see the thin line of the path that rose away into the trees at its edge.

'Where are we going?' said Darcy.

They stepped quietly away onto the cobbled surface.

'Morwenna's,' said Mawgan. 'Now, no more talking. We must be quick, and we must be quiet.' Mawgan grabbed Darcy's hand and with Kea and Glewas either side of them, they ran in the direction of Piddleton village and Morwenna.

The journey passed uneventfully, and an hour later, they saw the flickering lights of the village as they approached its outskirts. The village of Piddleton was small, just twenty homes, all of them thatched cottages arranged around a square along with a pub and a village store. There was a clock tower at the centre of the square. The houses, the pub and the shop, were all arranged in such a way that everyone could see all the comings and goings of the other inhabitants or any visitors they might have. All the houses were in darkness. The shop was deserted and closed. They could hear the sound of singing and rowdy voices coming from the pub.

'We'll never make it unseen,' said Glewas.

He looked across at Mawgan.

'It's too open, no cover.'

'An' too well lit,' said Kea.

'We'll have to risk it,' said Mawgan. 'If we keep close to the houses, we should be able to do it. Most people are in the pub by the sounds of it, and the homes are all in darkness. We may, if we are quiet, go unnoticed.'

'Maybe Morwenna is in the pub too,' said Darcy.

Kea, Glewas and Mawgan exchanged knowing looks.

'What's the matter?' said Darcy.

'She won't be in the pub, Darcy,' said Glewas. 'She isn't welcome in there...'

'Or pretty much anywhere,' Kea said. 'It's a witch thing, people is afraid o' witches.'

'Can we discuss this later?' Mawgan glared at them both. 'Get your minds back on the problem. We need to get to that house over there. The one in the farthest corner.'

Mawgan looked again into the emptiness of the village square.

'Now.'

Glewas grabbed Darcy's hand. With a quick nod at her, they started to pick their way through the village, going from one dark corner to another, skipping through those areas that were lit by streetlamps as quickly as they could. They made it to Morwenna's house and hid down the side of it in the darkness.

On seeing that Darcy and Glewas had made it successfully around the square, Mawgan and Kea began their run. They were halfway around when the pub door opened, spilling out three men. Kea and Mawgan hovered where they were, afraid to breathe, in a dimly lit doorway. The three men staggered their way across the square, the worse for drink they held each other up.

'Bye, Bill.'

Two of the men slurred as the third broke away, and to Mawgan and Kea's dismay began to wobble in their direction.

'Bye, Harry, George, see ya tomorra,'

Bill called back, stumbling as he reached the clock in the centre of the square and stopping for a moment. He put his hand out to steady himself before starting out again.

'He's comin' 'ere,' whispered Kea. 'We'll hav' to make a run fer it. 'Ee's gonna see us whatever we do.'

'You're right,' said Mawgan. 'We don't have a choice. Let's go.'

They ran from the doorway to the centre of the square. Kea gave Bill a hard shove as they passed him, Bill stumbled and fell to the ground, lying face down. Kea and Mawgan then dashed into the darkness of another doorway.

'Oi! Wha' did ya do that fer?' said Bill.

He farted loudly as he struggled to get back on his feet.

George and Harry, who were still wobbling along, arm in arm, at the other side of the square, turned to look at what was happening by the clock tower.

'Ah Bill, you're disgustin' you are.' said Harry

At seeing Bill struggling to right himself, George and Harry made their wobbly way over to him.

'What's goin' on Bill?' said George.

He had arrived by Bill's side and helped him up.

'Someone jus' knocked me over,' said Bill.

His red face was slack and a large globule of sweat ran off his nose

'There's no one 'ere Bill,' said Harry,

He looked about.

'You'd better lay off the booze a bit. You're startin' ta see things that jus' ain't there.'

'He pushed me over,' Bill insisted.

He brushed the dirt from his trousers, rocking back and forth with the motion.

'Na!' said George.

Studying Bill through bloodshot eyes.

'Ya jus' fell over. Get yerself 'ome an' sleep it off.'

The conversation in the village square had distracted the tree men enough to give Kea and Mawgan the time required to make it to Darcy and Glewas' hiding place. The four of them now watched Bill, George and Harry make their ways slowly, wobbling off in the direction of their homes.

'Phew!' said Glewas. 'That was close.'

'Close is not caught Glewas,' said Mawgan. 'Well done, Kea, you saved us from discovery by your quick thinking there.'

Darcy let out her breath. She was worried that even the slightest sound she could make would be overheard. Her hands were shaking. She clasped them together tightly to make them stop.

'What now?' she asked.

'Now we see Morwenna,' said Mawgan.

He slipped from the hiding place around to the front door and knocked.

Morwenna heard another knock on her front door and sighed.

'What do they want now?' she said.

She got up from her chair.

Was it going to be a sick pet this time? Or a child? Or someone wanting weed killer for their garden?

'Maybe it's that witch Tryfena back again? No, it couldn't be her, that one just lets herself in.'

Morwenna stomped towards the door, preparing herself for what she might find on the other side of it. It always amazed her that even though the other villagers were afraid of her, for some, she thought, it was more than that, as soon as there was a problem, they couldn't solve themselves, Morwenna would always find them on her doorstep.

She opened the door to find four people standing there. Three were strangers, the fourth she knew.

'Mawgan!'

'Please let us in Morwenna,' said Mawgan, 'quickly, we mustn't be seen.'

She stood aside and let them in. Before closing the door again, she looked up and down the square. The sound of singing was coming from the pub, but there was no one else about. Morwenna closed the door and walked into the living room.

'Please sit,' she said.

'I'll be standin' if it's all the same to 'ee,' said Kea.

He wrung his hands and paced up and down the room. Morwenna smiled.

'I won't hurt you.'

'No, but ya might jus' change me into a toad or weasel or somethin',' Kea replied. Morwenna laughed.

'Do you really think I can do that?'

'Oh Kea, just shut up and sit down.'

Darcy growled and moved to one side, indicating at a space on the sofa next to her. Kea slumped down on it.

'Where do they hear this stuff from?' Morwenna asked Mawgan.

'Gossip and rumours, none of it true, of course. But since when has the truth been important where there is a good story to be had or a person to vilify?'

He smiled at her.

'There is some information you have Morwenna that we are in need of.'

'Oh?' she replied.

'We need you to tell us how to get to the Vale of Secrets. More than that, we need to know how to survive the journey.'

'Oh,' said Morwenna again. 'Well, I think this call for some tea.'

A short while later, as they sat in the living room sipping at their tea; all of them that was except Kea, who would not accept anything to drink or eat and paced the floor still. Morwenna began her tale.

'I was a very young witch. My parents were strict and disapproving of my interest in the healing arts. That's really all witch's do you know.'

She addressed her statement at Kea in particular.

'We heal and help where we can, using what the earth provides and a bit of our own talent. My parents were much like you Kea, they didn't understand and became more and more afraid. They were frightened that my younger sister Jenna would follow my lead and become a witch too. Little did they know. One day, I came home from school to find the head of my village waiting for me. He told me that the time had come for me to leave, that there was no place here for a person like me. I pleaded with my parents to let me stay, but they turned their backs on me. Other men from our village came with dogs. They were outside my home; I remember being very frightened. I was pushed outside into the street. The men were angry, their dogs growled. They shouted at me, told me to go, to run away. I ran. As I reach the outskirts of the village, I heard the dogs. They were loose, and they were after me. I ran some more, but I wasn't fast enough, the dogs were gaining on me. I reached the oak wood just outside the village. It was dark under the enormous trees, and I hoped I would be harder to find, but I hadn't taken into account that dogs have very sensitive noses; they were following my scent. They were almost on me. I could hear them panting. I was exhausted, my legs felt like they were full of lead. I knew I was done for. My only hope would be if I could climb into one of the trees, high enough out of their reach, and hide in the canopy. I climbed, but I couldn't get my legs to work fast enough. I felt something sharp dig into my ankle, whatever it was ripped my skin. I screamed and lost my grip. After that, I don't remember anything more.'

The company listened to Morwenna's story. Nobody moved, Darcy's breath slowly hissed out from between her gappy teeth. Kea was the next to break the silence.

'What happened then?'

He had sat down again next to Darcy. His face was ashen, and his large eyes held a look that Darcy had never seen on him before. He leaned forward, urging Morwenna to go on. She sipped her tea, looked straight into Kea's eyes and continued.

'I don't really know. I woke up hours later, still lying on the ground. It was dark, and I was colder than I had ever been in my life. My leg was bleeding, and I had a cut on my head. I remember sitting up and feeling relief immediately that I was alone. The dogs and men had all gone. It was then as I sat there that it finally dawned on me I really was alone. I had no one and nowhere to go. I struggled up onto my feet and tried to walk, but my leg was so sore I couldn't manage it, so I just stood hugging a tree. The cold was making me sleepy, and my eyes wanted to close. I just wanted the sleep to take over, to take me away. I had never seen a pixie before that day, so I had no idea what to expect, or how powerful their brand of magic could be. But there they were now, right in front of me. They were huge, much bigger than I was. I later discovered it was Hicca who picked me up in his arms. I fainted. I remember though the feeling of warmth that came off him. I was frightened, but I was so exhausted that I fell asleep in his arms. He just carried me.'

Tears made their way down Morwenna's pale face as she remembered. Kea coughed. He got up from where he was sitting and walked across to her chair. His hand was shaking slightly as he placed it on her shoulder.

'I'm sorry,' he said.

Walking over to the tea tray, he poured himself a cup of very stewed tea.

'So?' said Glewas. 'You were picked up by the pixies. What happened after that?'

'I was out cold all night. When I finally regained consciousness, Hicca was still carrying me. The sky was growing light around us. My head ached, and my leg was throbbing. I couldn't seem to form words, I just cried. Hicca spoke softly with Nix next to him. I heard them discussing me and the fact that I needed my wounds tending to or they would go bad. I remember they discussed where they should take me, but neither one of them could decide what was best. In the end, it was Nix who suggested that they should take me home with them. I remember Hicca baulked at the idea at first, but quickly came to realise that there were no other options for me. They continued to carry me, taking turns. I don't remember very much about the journey. All I felt was sickness, my mind all over the place, with colours and strange sounds, I couldn't concentrate on anything. There was the sensation that I was flying, but I don't know if that was real or imagined. It grew dark and light twice more so we must have travelled for three days before we made it to the Vale, I Couldn't tell you in what direction we travelled.'

'What about the Vale of Secrets?' Glewas asked. 'Tell us about it.'

Morwenna looked down at her hands folded in her lap.

'I can't speak about that place. I made a promise, and I have never broken it.'

'We wouldn't want you to do that now,' said Mawgan with a stern look at Glewas to not push the subject.

Morwenna continued, 'I made a promise not to speak of it. The pixies are very secretive. They have survived as long as they have because no one has ever seen or found the Vale and I promised I would not put them in danger. Anyway, I couldn't tell you how to find it. I don't know. When I go there, it just happens, I never remember how to do it after I've left. That's just the way their magic works and its kept them safe for many, many years.'

'So, all this messin' about has been fer nothin' then.'

Kea could not disguise the disappointment in his voice, nor the accompanying look on his face.

'Not necessarily,' Mawgan said. 'Morwenna cannot speak of the Vale, but there are two pixies that are known to us. They know very well how to find the Vale. They have already taken a human there, so perhaps they would do the same again if circumstances warranted it.'

'The last time I saw Nix and Hicca,' said Darcy, 'Hicca was so sick. We don't even know if he survived. No one's seen them since that night. How would we even contact them?'

'Morwenna' Mawgan said.

She lifted her eyes and looked directly at him.

'I will call the Pixies,' she answered.

Mawgan looked pleased with himself. He had got them safely to Morwenna's home, and now he'd had his suspicions confirmed.

Morwenna and the Pixies were communicating. More than that, she could speak to them at will. That was the best news by far he had come across today.

'Let's get some food, then we should all rest,' Morwenna suggested. 'Mawgan. Tryphena's been here, she knew to look for you, we can't risk you being here too long, you'll need to keep moving.'

'We will also need you to come with us,' Mawgan replied. 'Not just because of contacting the Pixies, but also as it will not be safe for you to stay either. Narcasta knew we would come to you. He will have you watched and if he suspects anything he will have you taken to the castle.'

Although Morwenna considered herself generally capable of handling anything Narcasta or his servants could throw her way, she understood there were more people than just herself to consider now. For the first time in a very long time, she felt she was not alone. She had a purpose. It filled her with excitement and fear all at once. Keeping her emotions under control was difficult as she worked with her four guests, preparing food, but she managed it. They prepared not just for a quick meal now, but also for their travels, wherever they might take them. While they worked, they planned. They then ate in silence, each alone with their own thoughts. Darcy's jaw was rigid. It was the face she always made when she was fixed on something. She tried to rest for a few hours as Mawgan had suggested, but sleep evaded her. She rolled from side to side, back and forth, but she was more awake than ever.

Mawgan woke the others. It was time to leave. As they crept out of the back door of Morwenna's cottage, the clock in the square struck 3am.

The morning was black and silent. The lightest footsteps on the path sounded as if they were being made by a giant. They crept along, making for the road out of Piddleton. Just as they were approaching the outskirts of the village, they heard heavy footsteps on the path behind them. The group picked up their speed, but the faster they went, the faster the steps behind seemed to get, and closer. The road passed through the dense wood that ran down to the Willow's home.

'Here we go at last.' said Mawgan. 'We'll split up from here, Darcy, you are with me, the rest of you, get yourselves lost and do the same with whoever is following us.'

Mawgan grabbed Darcy and pulled her along beside him. Under the trees, it was so dark. Darcy's fingers pulsed with the ache of coldness. Mawgan squeezed them in his own hand, and she yelped with the pain. They could hear footsteps to the left and right. Darcy didn't know if it was Kea, Morwenna or Glewas or if it was someone or something else entirely.

'Come on, we have to go faster,' said Mawgan.

They ran, darting here and there, never keeping to a straight path, doubling back, pushing forward, always moving. Twigs and branches scratched Darcy's face and caught in her coat. She stumbled on a tree root, Mawgan pulled her back onto her feet.

'We must keep going,' he said, 'they are very close.'

Suddenly there were little bursts of sound all around them. A titter here, a giggle there, a screech, and the rustling of leaves.

'Imps!' said Mawgan, 'damn them.'

They heard a yell.

'Ouch, you bugger.'

That could only have been from Kea. He sounded close. Darcy had an unexpected sense of reassurance at that. Something flew past her ear. Only after it whizzed past Darcy realised it was an Imp. Kea had thrown it off. Still running, she came up against a fallen tree trunk. It was only as Darcy was clambering over it, scratching her hands on the bark in the process, that she realised she had no idea where Mawgan was. She was afraid to stop, to look for him, but the urge to do so was too great. Whirling around, desperately trying to make out any shape in the darkness, she ended up smacking into the back of someone. Thrown off-balance, she stumbled and fell, hitting the ground hard, her chin scaped the rough surface. Darcy wiped it with the back of her hand, feeling the warmness of blood. There was a crack above her head, and light appeared to envelope her. There in the centre of the light, looming up over her, was Tryfena. Her arm held high above, manipulating the light with her hand, coaxing and controlling it.

'Got you.'

Tryfena's crackly voice came at Darcy like a slap in the face. The wood was silent around them. The light Tryfena had created seemed to eat any noise and darkness. It consumed it like food. Darcy felt heavy, suppressed. She tried to raise her arms, but she couldn't move. Small, dark faces appeared at the edge of the light. They glowed in the light with a deep blueish tinge. Darcy knew they must be the Imps; she saw the black light of their eyes and the rows of serrated teeth. Their faces were set in an ironic look of joy as they salivated. Their mouths still drooled the blood of their last victims. Slowly, they crept forward towards her.

'Oh no, you don't.'

Morwenna's voice came out of the darkness to Darcy's left. The light shifted to illuminate her. The Imps also turned their attention, following it. With little bursts of delight, they leapt at Morwenna. She was suddenly covered in a sea of writhing blackness. Horrified at what she saw, but also realising that this might be her only chance, Darcy found her feet and scrambled away. She ducked down behind the fallen tree trunk. She was desperate to help Morwenna, but she hadn't a clue how to do that. Darcy felt someone grab at her hand. She squealed and grabbed it away. The adrenalin in her body made her blind to the familiar face. Glewas, realising that Darcy was not in control, whispered reassuringly.

'It's ok, take it easy, you're fine. It's me.'

Once he was sure she was ok, he left her to deal with the more urgent matter of helping Morwenna. Glewas ran towards Morwenna and the black mass of Imps that now covered every part of her body. His face exploded with rage. Glewas grabbed at the first Imp, pulling it free and sending it flying off into the darkness behind him. He quickly did the same with the second, third and fourth Imps which followed the first, squealing he sent them flying into the dark. There were several thwacks as they hit tree trunks and the ground, and then silence. After what seemed an age to Darcy but could only have been a few seconds, Glewas pulled the last Imp off Morwenna and sent it flying into the night. Darcy found the use of her legs, although still a bit wobbly, she made her way to where Morwenna was lying, Glewas was bending low over Morwenna's limp body. She was so pale, little bite marks were visible all over her neck, face and arms. Darcy knelt by her, took her hand and felt how cold and lifeless it was in hers.

'Oh no, no,' she kept repeating.

The tears welling up in her eyes and spilling down her cheeks, her shoulders heaved up and down with the sobs as they came. Kea rushed up to them and stopped short. He bent his head in a solemn moment of respectful grief, looking down at where Morwenna lay motionless. Behind them in the blackness an almighty crack like thunder sounded, followed in quick succession by a shot of light that split the air above them. A scream of hate–filled pain cut into the night. In that second Darcy knew it had been made by Tryfena, and Mawgan was the cause.

Distracted by what was going on behind them, Darcy, Glewas and Kea had failed to notice that Morwenna had slipped her hand from Darcy's and was slowly rubbing at the itchy little bite marks on her face and neck. She made a soft moaning sound, Darcy looked down at her. The tears still running from her eyes splashed onto Mowenna's coat.

'You're alive,' she whispered.

Mawgan then stumbled through the darkness to where they were all kneeling now beside Morwenna.

'Come on,' he said. 'We need to get somewhere safe and quickly, they are gone for now, but they will be back, and the dawn is not far away.'

'What happened to that old woman?' asked Darcy.

'I've taken care of her for now,' said Mawgan, 'but you can be sure that Narcasta will send others. Come on, let's go.'

They helped Morwenna slowly to her feet. She was very unsteady and Glewas, and Kea held her upright between them.

'It's not far,' Mawgan said, 'follow me.'

They moved, slowly now, through the wood. The light increased. Dawn was here. They could make out the shadowy shapes of the trees. The wood was comfortingly silent. Mawgan halted in front of a small bushy clump of hawthorn. Pushing his way through, he disappeared.

'Go on, Darcy,' Glewas encouraged.

She noticed a little break in the foliage and stepped on through, closing her eyes to shield them from any stray branches. Her hands held out in front of her were suddenly in open space. She opened her eyes. Surprisingly, she was now in a large cave. She was nearly knocked over by Glewas and Kea as they stepped through behind her, helping Morwenna along between them.

'Wow!' Kea exclaimed.

'Wow, indeed,' said Glewas.

The cave was a vast limestone cavern. Its soaring roof was covered with stalactites that slowly dripped milky white coloured water onto the stalagmites growing on the floor below, yet there was nothing cold and damp about this place. Glass and brass lanterns scattered here and there cast ghostly shadows onto the walls that appeared to dance as candles inside flickered. Someone had carved a few of the stalagmites into furniture, a chair, a table. Several crevices in the walls, on closer inspection, revealed themselves to contain beds, with deep filled mattresses, topped with fluffy pillows and eiderdowns. A fire blazed in a hearth which had been hewn from the rock of the cave itself. Its fiery reflection was mirrored in a pool that covered half the cave floor; its depth could only be guessed at as its bottom disappeared into blackness. One wall was covered with shelves from floor to roof. The shelves contained all manner of fruit, vegetables, packets and filled baskets of bread, flour, corn and any amount of herbs and spices to cook with. Pots and pans were strewn about the shelves along with books and other items, their uses yet to be determined.

Darcy stood still, taking everything in. The place had an unordinary sense of peace. Glewas and Kea pushed past her, still carrying Morwenna between them. They moved across the cave to a bed and gently laid Morwenna on it, Mawgan began to tend to her. Darcy moved to see if she could help.

'Will she be ok?' she asked.

'I think so,' Mawgan replied, 'she needs rest and a little food to help her replace the blood she's lost, but she's alive, and her heart is strong, she will mend. Let's leave her now to rest. We can eat, and then I think we could all do with some sleep.'

Darcy was suddenly aware of her own exhaustion. She had been running on pure adrenaline, and now there was nothing more left in her. She reached up and covered her suddenly gaping mouth with her hand. Her eyes watered with the effort of it. Glewas and Kea were over at the table, noisily delving into the bags and laying out sandwiches, cold meat and biscuits they had prepared earlier at Morwenna's. Darcy and Mawgan joined them. They ate, Morwenna even managed a few mouthfuls too before falling back to sleep. Darcy turned to Mawgan.

'Will we be safe here? I mean, will they find us?'

Darcy's forehead contracted into long furrows that ran right across from one side to the other. Mawgan reached out and took her hand in his. He smiled and patted it.

'No one will find us here, Darcy. This place has been in my family for generations. There is deep magic here, it sings in the plants and trees, it even rings in these old cave walls.'

Darcy closed her eyes and tried to focus her ears.

'It protects and preserves the cave and anyone within it.'

She shook her head. She heard nothing.

'Is this your home then Mawgan?' she asked,

realising that she really knew very little about him.

'Yes,' he said. 'I grew up here. It was my protection while I was young and too inexperienced to do that myself, and now it will safeguard us all.'

Tired, Darcy crept to the small space in the wall that was her bed and sunk into the soft downy mattress. Within seconds she had fallen fast asleep.

Much later, her eyes flickered open. She breathed in deeply. The air hung with a sweet mustiness. It wasn't a nasty smell; instead, it was intensely comforting, a safe smell. She sat up; the cave was very quiet. The others were all sleeping. Darcy crept out of bed, drank some water from a flask and nibbled on a biscuit she pinched off the table. Wandering over to the wall of shelves, she looked up and down the many rows. There were so many books. Her eyes settled on a leather-bound one lying on its side. Reaching it down, she turned it over in her hands. It had gilt edges that glistened in the light; the cover was stamped with many small pictures. As Darcy inspected them more closely, she realised they were more like symbols than pictures. Inside, the pages were filled with more of the same. She thought it maybe was some sort of writing, but nothing like she had seen before.

'They're runes,' a quiet voice said behind her.

Darcy turned around to see Morwenna. Her scratched feet were bare on the cold stone floor.

'Where are your shoes?'

Morwenna still looked pale and quite fragile, but there was something in her eyes that had not been there before. It was a deep intensity; it made Darcy nervous, and she looked away.

'It's ok Darcy, I did it for you so you could get away and it worked.'

'I should have helped you; I shouldn't have left you there by yourself.'

'No!' said Morwenna. 'If you had been caught, it would have all been for nothing. We all knew what we were getting into. These were our decisions to make Darcy. You have nothing to feel bad about.'

Darcy looked again at Morwenna. She was smiling now.

'You met my sister in Bude,' Morwenna said, 'Mawgan told me. How was she?'

'She was very helpful and kind,' said Darcy, 'she gave me this.'

Darcy lifted her rucksack off the table, reaching in she retrieved the colourful patchwork bag and handed it to Morwenna. Tipping its contents out onto the table, Morwenna smiled.

'Darcy, did you look at what's in this bag?'

'No,' she replied, 'I was afraid I would break something.'

Two small green lights shot in through the entrance at the mouth of the cave and came to a stop a few feet from Darcy and Morwenna. In a flash of green, the lights transformed into Hicca and Nix, full-sized. Nix ran to Morwenna and hugged her tight. Taking her face in her hands and stroking her dark head.

'Are 'ee alrigh' me darlin'? Did they hurt 'ee?'

The commotion soon had all the cave's occupants wide awake. Everyone was suddenly out of bed, wanting to know what was going on. Morwenna was busy calming Nix down, reassuring her she was okay. Hicca had taken a seat at the table. Mawgan sat down beside him.

'It's good to see you Hicca, you are better, I trust?'

'I'm well Mawgan, thank 'ee. It were touch 'n go there fer a bit, but Nix got me through. How is she?'

Hicca looked across at Morwenna, who was still enduring all the fuss from Nix.

'She's strong,' said Mawgan, 'like you.'

Hicca smiled and looked down at the table where Morwenna had tipped out the contents of Jenna's bag.

'Look at this?' he said.

Holding up a small, round, gold object for Mawgan.

'A compass?'

CHAPTER SEVEN

THE COMPASS

The compass's copper case shone in Hicca's hand as he held it up in the light. It was covered in runic symbols that changed and flickered depending on how the light caught them; like a lenticular picture does as you move it from side to side. Hicca grasped at the little clasp and pressed it. The case sprung open. It had an ornate dial that looked like it had been taken from the legend of an ancient map. North, South, East and West were clearly set at equal quarters around the dial, but the pointer spun continuously, never settling on a particular direction, always moving.

'What's that?' asked Darcy.

She had moved to see what Hicca and Mawgan were examining.

'It's a compass' said Mawgan, 'and I'd like to know where exactly you got it?'

His eyebrows drew together, making a deep line down the middle of his wrinkled forehead.

'I don't know,' said Darcy, 'I've never seen it before.'

She returned Mawgan's gaze with one so innocently blank that he immediately knew she was telling the truth.

'She didn't know, but she had it all along,' said Morwenna. 'Jenna must have packed it for her. Darcy never looked into the bag until I tipped it out onto the table, just before you arrived Hicca, she was too afraid of it.'

'Hmmm,' said Mawgan, his face still wrinkled with frowning. Darcy thought that if the wind changed direction, he just might stay that way forever.

'So much time wasted; ah well, let's not waste anymore.'

With that he took the compass from Hicca and dangling it from a chain, he placed it over Darcy's head. As soon as Darcy felt the weight of it on her neck, the pointer stopped spinning and settled on North East.

'Woah!' said Hicca, 'look wha' it did.'

'That's exactly how it's supposed to work,' said Mawgan, 'you have to wear it to use it.'

Darcy looked down at the compass and traced a finger over the casing. Everyone stood looking at her. She lifted her head. Tears sparkled on the rims of her eyelids.

'I can go home,' she said.

Mawgan placed a hand on her shoulder.

'Yes, Darcy, you can.'

They stayed in Mawgan's cave for a week. Morwenna grew stronger every day, the colour came back to her cheeks, and Nix's fussing over her became less as she returned to her usual self.

'Nix fusses around you like my mother does around me,' said Darcy.

They were sat at the table examining the compass with the book of runes spread out between them.

'Nix and Hicca are my parents, really,' said Morwenna. 'When I left home, I was so young. If they hadn't found me that day in the woods, I don't know what would have happened to me. They took me in and cared for me until I was old enough to do that myself. It was no small thing that they did. I can handle a little fussing now and then, I'm very grateful to them.'

'What happened to your sister after you left?' said Darcy. 'She must have been frightened that the same thing would happen to her.'

'I was away a very long time; Jenna and I grew up apart. She always was so much smarter than I was, she found better ways to keep what she is hidden. My parents never knew Jenna was a witch until the day she left them, I'm not sure if they fully understood even then. This compass must be hers; I don't know where she got it, I never knew she had one until now. But thinking about it, it's obvious really, Jenna must have used one to travel through to your world Darcy, she would have known you would need it too.'

Darcy looked down at the compass around her neck, lifting it she felt its weight in her hands.

'Why does Jenna stay on the other side and not come back? She had a compass; she could have done it.'

Morwenna stopped flicking through the book pages and looked directly at Darcy.

'She's wanted by Narcasta. He collects people, mostly those with magic. Jenna went away, so she didn't have to make that choice. It's no choice, really. Once Narcasta has chosen you, that's it. So, she can't come back, not now.'

The night they left Mawgan's cave, it was silent and still. Their breath hung in the air as wispy clouds before slowly drifting away. The seven made their way as quietly as they could, trying to achieve the impossibility of silently walking over the leaves and branches to the outskirts of Willow Wood. Kea stopped walking and looked in another direction, into the wood. Darcy could not fathom the look on his face at that moment. It was so strange, like he knew something that no one else did. Glewas put a hand on his shoulder.

'We'll be back,' he said.

'Ugh, yeah.' said Kea.

Glewas's eyes narrowed slightly.

Darcy suddenly understood. They must be near Trecath-en. In the dark, she had not recognised anything at all, but to Kea, this place was as familiar as his favourite pair of socks. As they reached the edge of the wood, the going was becoming easier. The trees thinned, and the light from the moon lit their path. Abruptly the wood came to an end. Stretched out before them like an enormous patchwork in the dark were the miles and miles of farmland that Darcy remembered from the day she had arrived and fallen through the hedge onto an unsuspecting Kea. Mawgan drew them all to a stop.

'It should be easier going from here,' he said. 'Easier to be seen too, so keep your eyes peeled and your wits about you. Oh, and keep the noise down, it's like travelling with a herd of elephants.'

They climbed the stile over the fence to the first field. It was full of barley. Darcy could hear her parent's past discussions on ancient farming practices, and how barley was an ancient grain, one of the first to be grown deliberately by people thousands of years ago. In that moment, they were very close. The sweet smell of mud mixed with grass and sweat filled her nostrils. It was their smell. It was home. She closed her eyes and let the scent linger for as long as she could hold on to it.

'Heh hem.'

Mawgan was behind her on the stile.

Darcy had never seen barley so high. Once she hopped down amongst it, she was completely covered. It was a good few inches taller than she was and smelled of musty beer. They walked on, following the access path the farmer had conveniently left for his machinery until they came to the next field. On and on they went through the night, from field to field. Every hour or so, Mawgan checked the compass around Darcy's neck. It still pointed North East, and so they continued.

Eventually, the night sky gave in to the first signs of watery light approaching. It changed from midnight blue to indigo, then to a pink-tinged navy. They came to another fence. This time on the other side was a holding yard with corralled areas to hold cattle before they were moved somewhere else. Pieces of machinery were parked here and there. On one side stood the farmhouse, still and dark in the early morning, and over in the far corner stood a big double storey barn. Mawgan turned to the group.

'We need to get inside before it becomes too light. The barn over there looks promising.'

'We'll check it out.' Hicca said.

He and Nix shrunk and sped across the open space between the fenced field and the barn; once there, they shot in through an open window. A few minutes later, they were back.

'The barns empty,' Nix said, 'jus' some odds and ends of machinery downstairs, upstairs is a hayloft, 'ee should be fine up there.'

'Ok,' said Glewas, 'let's go.'

They made their way across the yard. Halfway between the fields and the barn the door to the farmhouse swung open and out came a burly man who pointed the shotgun he was carrying straight at them.

'An' jus' what might you lot be doin' on my land?' He asked.

His voice reminded Darcy of scraping shoes over rough gravel. Mawgan spread his arms and gathered them all behind him like a great mother bird.

'We just need shelter,' he said. 'We mean no harm to you or your family. We were hoping just to sleep in your hayloft a while, that's all.'

The farmer looked at the group more closely. What a strange lot they were. Two boys, a girl, a young woman and an old man—Nix and Hicca had disappeared again—they didn't look dangerous, but you never could tell these days. Still, it wasn't in his nature to be unfriendly.

'Well, 'ee better come in then, Mrs Tussock would never let me 'ere the end of it if I turn 'ee all out now would she.'

He put the gun down and walked back into the house.

'Come on with ya' don't be takin' all day abou' it.'

He beckoned them with an arm gesture.

On entering the house, they were greeted by the smell of eggs and bacon sizzling on the stove. Breakfast was cooking. A large round woman was speaking in whispers with her husband while working the eggs and bacon around the pan. She stopped and looked at her guests.

'Sit 'eeselves down me lovelies, 'ee looks famished do the lot of 'ees.'

Indicating for them to sit at the table, she handed out plates, knives and forks. She put bread, butter and several types of jam in front of them, and then went back to the stove to carry on with the bacon and eggs.

By the time they had finished their breakfast, it was completely light outside. The sun warmed the room, and bird song drifted in through the open window. Darcy's eyes began to droop, and she slumped a bit in her chair.

'Look at the poor love,' said Mrs Tussock. 'She's fair jiggered, that she is.'

'Yes, mam,' said Mawgan, 'we all are.'

'I don't have beds for all of 'ee,' said Mrs Tussock.

'We won't be needing your beds,' said Mawgan. 'Your hayloft will be just fine for us. Thank you.'

After relaying their thanks to the Tussocks, they made their way across the yard and into the barn. Up in the hayloft, Nix and Hicca were already asleep. The others soon joined them.

They slept on into the late afternoon; the sun crept low towards the horizon. A distant black speck was visible just above it. The speck was growing as Mr Tussock stood watching it.

'I wonder wha' tha' could be?' He said to himself as he worked on the plough.

'Ere Ma,' he called into the open kitchen window. 'Wha do 'ee make of that?'

Mrs Tussock bundled out of the kitchen door, wiping her hands on the front of her floral apron, and squinted at the speck Mr Tussock was pointing at. She clasped the front of her dress and cardigan at her chest and reached out to hold the plough handle as her legs collapsed beneath her. Mr Tussock swung round and just about caught her in his arms.

'Marnie, Marnie, wha' is it, love? Wha's wrong?'

She looked up at him. Her soft, plump face contorted into the most terrified expression.

'B–b–buzzards,' she said.

Mr Tussock helped his wife back indoors and into the nearest chair.

'Stay 'ere,' he said.

Grabbing his shotgun, he ran to the barn.

'Wake up, wake up all of 'ee's.'

Glewas was the first to stir and popped his head over the top of the ladder.

'What's up?'

He rubbed at his eyes, trying to focus them. Then he noticed the shotgun. Mawgan joined Glewas, looking down the ladder at the farmer.

'What's the matter?'

'Buzzards,' was all Tussock said.

Glewas and Mawgan woke everyone quickly. Mr Tussock climbed the ladder to the hayloft. On hearing his feet climbing the runs, Nix and Hicca disappeared out of a small hatch window. As he reached the ladder's last rung, Glewas finally woke Kea, who muttered something unintelligible and sat up, rubbing his eyes. Mr

Tussock moved quickly to the far corner of the hayloft. There, he swept aside the dry hay and lifted a trapdoor.

'In 'ere,' he said. 'Quickly now.'

They scrambled for their few possessions, and quickly as they could, climbed down through the hatch into what they soon discovered was a hidden room below.

'I hide things in 'ere I want to keep from Narcasta. Right now that's 'ee, so quiet, not a sound.'

Once they were all safely inside, Mr Tussock closed the hatch on them and recovered it with hay. He did a final check that they had left nothing incriminating behind in the loft before he retreated down the ladder. Once outside, he propped the gun against a wheel of the plough, close enough to grab. He looked up at the three buzzards, clearly visible now and not far away. Also visible, riding on the back of the biggest bird, he could see the bulky form of Barrowman.

Enormous wings could be heard outside, and Darcy shivered involuntarily. She held her breath, afraid it would make a sound, and clenched her hands tight in her lap to stop them shaking. Darcy felt Glewas' hand on hers. He took it in his, smiling at her in encouragement. She smiled weakly back and then returned to the task of trying to be still and quiet. With her hands in Glewas' her heart seemed to be beating outside of her chest, she was convinced everyone would hear. Outside though, the noise of wings was replaced by snapping beaks and shrill bird calls. The buzzards had landed.

'What you doin' 'ere Barrowman?' said Mr Tussock.

He didn't look up from his work on the plough.

'We're in search of a party,' said Barrowman. 'They may have come this way through your fields, have you seen anyone unusual lately, anyone a bit different, dressed for the road?'

'Don't see anyone,' said Tussock. 'Don't hear abou' anyone. Nobody comes through 'ere, and we're too busy to have visitors.'

Mr Tussock glanced at the gun propped beside him. Had he remembered to load it? Barrowman looked suspiciously around the yard and slid down off the back of the great bird.

'Well, if you don't mind,' he continued, 'I'd like to look around and check for myself.'

'Go ahead,' Tussock muttered, still not looking up from the plough.

Barrowman walked towards the barn, and Tussock slid his hand to the gun. All in the barn was silent and still. Barrowman looked around at the scattered odds and ends of machinery and then climbed the ladder to the loft. Hearing his steps as he crossed the floor above them, Darcy, Glewas, Morwenna, Kea and Mawgan sat like statues, barely breathing. Barrowman was very close now. Darcy looked upwards at the trapdoor.

What if he stood on it?

He would surely know what it was, and they would be discovered. An almighty howl coming from behind him made Barrowman swing around. The farm cat streaked across the hayloft floor and jumped out through the window. It had been spooked by the buzzards outside and now landing on its feet was tearing headlong towards the farms outlying barley fields. Barrowman took another look around the barn. His heavy footfall sounded above Darcy's head. Inch by inch, it was getting closer to the door. One more step and it would be all over. Darcy held her breath and squeezed her eyes tight shut till they ached.

One more, just one more.

He turned, made his way down the ladder and outside again.

Mr Tussock was still pretending to work on the plough as Barrowman walked towards him.

'Like I said Barrowman, nothin' going on 'ere,' he said. 'Ain't seen no one in weeks, busy time of year tryin' to get all this grain in, the wife's fair jiggered with it all that she is. She's restin', and I don't want 'ee goin' on in there disturbin' 'er.'

Tussock motioned with a hand towards the farmhouse.

'Ok Tussock, we'll be on our way,' said Barrowman. 'But I'll hear of it if you have been lying to me and that shotgun of yours, it will be of no use to you, believe me.'

The tone in Barrowman's voice was unmistakable. Tussock knew he was taking a risk, but there was something about those people. He couldn't really tell what it was, but he seemed to know the risk was worth the taking. With another swift look around the farmyard, Barrowman climbed again onto the back of the enormous beast.

'Come on.'

He jabbed at the bird cruelly with spurs that protruded from the heels of his black boots. It squawked in protest and flapped its wings. Following the first bird, all the buzzards took to the air and flew off in the direction of the barley fields and Willow wood.

Tussock rushed into the house to check on his wife. She was still in the chair where he had put her, shaking.

'It's alrigh' love,' he said. 'They're gone.'

She took his hand in hers and kissed it in relief.

'What a-abou' them there kids in our barn?' she stammered.

'All safe, my love,' he said. 'We should feed 'em and get 'em on their way, it's not safe for 'em to stay.'

Tussock raised the trapdoor above Mawgan's head. They crept out of the cramped space, one by one, glad to stand upright again. Darcy unravelled herself, muscle by muscle. As she finally straightened up, she realised she was still holding Glewas's hand.

'Mrs Tussocks got some food on the go fer 'ee,' said Tussock. 'Then 'ee should get goin', it'll be dark soon.'

Everyone made their way across the yard and back into the farmhouse.

'We can't thank you enough,' said Mawgan, 'and for the hospitality of your table.'

'Any enemy of Narcasta's is a friend of ours,' said Tussock. 'I don't know why he wants 'ee, or where 'ee's are goin', but I wish 'ee well with it.'

Mawgan shook Tussock's hand, and they left.

The moon was visible again above the barley fields. They walked through the night. Field after field they crossed, not speaking, only stopping occasionally to check the compass and that they were still heading North East. Nix and Hicca re-joined them as the first watery rays of morning sunlight broke over the horizon.

'How come 'ee always disappear when the action starts?' said Kea.

He smirked.

'Ee worry abou' 'eeself Kea Willow,' said Hicca, 'an' Nix and I will do what we 'ave to do.'

As he said this, the group found themselves brought to a sudden halt. The field of barley they were crossing dropped away. They were standing on a cliff edge, below them was the sea. It shimmered beautifully in the early light. Darcy noticed the mast of the tall ship first, its mainsail caught her eye as it fluttered in its ties.

'Well done, Hicca,' Mawgan exclaimed. 'Just what we want and right where you said it would be.'

The ship was a clipper, an ocean-going boat. Darcy had seen a similar boat in London when she had visited the Cutty Sark with her parents. This one was called The Lady Karensa. Its figurehead was a beautiful young woman with long flowing auburn hair, her white gown slashed to the waist so that it revealed one bare breast. She seemed totally unperturbed by this and stared regally out to sea. As they climbed aboard, Morwenna turned to Darcy and whispered:

'If only we all could be brave like that.'

Darcy nodded, giggling, while secretly thinking to herself that she didn't know of many who could look as pretty as Morwenna did today, her ebony hair blowing in the sea breeze that had also brought a pinkness to her usually pale cheeks.

Mawgan spoke with the captain to see if passage up the coast could be arranged. The captain was unsure if he could accommodate so many, but when he saw the gold coins that Mawgan produced from the capacious pocket in his cloak, he soon changed his mind and busied his crew in finding appropriate places for them all to sleep. Darcy and Morwenna were given the captain's staterooms, far away from the other sleeping quarters and any unwanted interest from the all-male crew. The boys and Mawgan had to make the best of a hammock each, bunked up with the rest. They were so tired it didn't matter much, falling asleep almost instantly. Morwenna and Darcy too fell asleep quickly. The captain's apartments were sumptuous and extremely comfortable, no luxury had been spared. The only members of the group not asleep were Nix and Hicca who took up a post in the crow's nest, high above the deck, keeping watch. As the sun rose, and as the company slept, the ship was underway, sailing up the coast.

Keeping out of sight of the shore but hugging the coast as tightly as the captain would dare, they made good headway. The wind filled the sails, and the boat sliced quickly through the waves. Still, in the crow's nest, Nix turned to Hicca.

'Wha's wrong with 'ee?' she asked.

Hicca had become as green as his tunic.

'Seasick,' said Hicca. He lent over the side and threw up. 'Aww, I feel terrible.'

He straightened up again, holding onto the side of the crow's nest for support. Below, a very confused sailor was looking around for the creator of the disgusting mess that had just landed on his head and the deck. High above, Hicca lent over the side of the crow's nest, ready to deliver another spew of vomit onto the unsuspecting sailor below.

As late afternoon approached, the rest of the group stirred from their sleeping places. Not long after waking, the boys and Mawgan were back on the deck, enjoying an animated conversation on just how fast the ship was.

'Must be fifty knots at least,' said Glewas.

'No, you're wrong,' said Kea. 'It'll only be abou' thirty, it always feels faster than it is.'

As Glewas and Kea argued, Mawgan was watching for any signs they were being followed or worse, pursued. Meanwhile, Morwenna and Darcy were taking advantage of a more leisurely approach to awaking. They lay on their beds, chatting.

'So, you and Glewas, what's going on there?' said Morwenna.

Darcy's forehead took on its usual furrows as her eyebrows raised and drew together.

'I don't know what you're talking about' she said.

'Don't you,' said Morwenna. It was more of a statement than a question. 'I've seen the way you look at him when you think no one else will notice, he's not exactly shy around you either. Took your hand when we were all stuck in that hayloft, didn't he?'

'You think so, you think he really does like me?' said Darcy, sitting up in bed.

Morwenna smiled.

'See,' she said. 'I knew it, I knew you liked him.'

Darcy threw her pillow across the room, and it hit Morwenna square on the head. Laughter burst out of her. It was as uncontrollable as the look of surprise on Morwenna's face. Darcy laughed until her sides ached, and her eyes watered. She laughed, and all the fear and tension of the last couple of weeks left with every burst.

Morwenna smiled again.

'Yes, Darcy, I think he likes you very much. But be careful, wizards can be strange, even cruel at times. They are capable of charming the birds out of the trees one moment and then as cold as an ice cube the next. It's part of who they are, it's their kind of magic, their charm, you could say. Anyway, that's enough of a warning, you probably won't listen, I can see he has you completely under his spell already.'

Darcy crossed her eyes and stuck out her tongue.

'Come on,' Morwenna said, laughing. 'We had better get up to the deck, the others will be awake too, and I wouldn't want you to miss out on any Glewas time.'

Laughing together, they made their way to join the rest. At the sight of Glewas, Darcy blushed, remembering.

Everyone was happy. It was a strange happiness. The ship seemed to cast a spell of wellbeing over them all. It was beautiful, and they felt safe. When evening came, they ate a meal at the captain's table. Shellfish cooked to perfection, followed by a soufflé that would have made the most accomplished French chef weep with joy, after which Darcy and Glewas stood together looking out to sea. Neither spoke, they just watched as the sun set on the horizon. Darcy looked down into the bright green water. As she did so, she saw a flash of silver. It caught in the sun's rays and was clearly visible in the depths below for a moment before it was gone again. There was another, and another, quick shimmers that melted away as quickly as they appeared.

'What's that?' she said.

'What's what?'

'That.'

Glewas followed her finger as she pointed into the water.

'Well, I never,' he said, 'Merfolk.'

'You're joking,' said Darcy.

'Nothing to joke about,' said Glewas. 'They're Eastern Merfolk to be accurate. Different races of Merpeople live in different oceans, just the same as with people living in different countries.'

A splash to their left had the rest of the company who had been milling around the deck, walking off their dinner, rushing to look over the side.

'Ah,' Mawgan said. 'So they have come.'

The ship slowed. Darcy looked above her as the crew scrambled up and down the rigging, gathering in the sails. Eventually, just as the last of the sun disappeared beyond the horizon, the boat came to a small inlet. The company was ushered into a launch and Kea, and Glewas, at Mawgan's instruction, rowed them out into the centre of the channel where a sandbank was forming. A few large rocks were visible now too as the tide was lowering.

'What are we doing?' said Darcy.

'It seems that Mawgan wants to talk with the Merfolk about something,' said Morwenna. 'This is a meeting place, not really land and not really sea, neutral, I think you'd call it.'

The launch pulled up on the sandbank, and they all got out. A soft cooing could be heard all around them. Was it a signal? It was. A moment later the company was surrounded by heads bobbing in the surf. Darcy's image of mermaids she had read about in stories was nothing like the real thing. These were sleek and scaled like a fish, their hair, well, what looked like hair, was really an extension of their bodies and formed a fin–like appendage at the back of their heads. Their faces, thin and pointed with flaps that were gills, positioned where a human's ears would typically be. Darcy stared, and then realising what she was doing, she looked away; she didn't want to appear rude. What could only be described as a giggle came from a merperson close by. This seemed to relax everyone.

'Heh hem,' said Mawgan, 'thank you for meeting with us.'

He addressed the large Merwoman in the centre of the bobbing group. The Merwoman nodded, so Mawgan continued.

'We are journeying in search of a door to the other world.'

The Merfolk gurgled excitedly.

'We have a compass.'

On hearing this, the Merfolk became even more excited. The Merwoman moved forward, closer to the sandbank.

'We are following it North East, up the coast.'

A voice that was clear enough to understand yet was strange and watery spoke.

'Has it changed its direction yet?'

The Merwoman was now just a few feet away. Darcy saw that her eyes glowed yellow, the enormous iris's able to take advantage of every speck of light available.

Mawgan was puzzled.

'Why would it do that?' he said. 'It leads to a door, aren't the doors fixed?'

'No,' the Merwoman gurgled. 'They move, that's why there is need of a compass to show their whereabouts. Mostly they move because they are in danger of discovery or if there is a shift in a timeline, but there is a good chance that you will need to follow more than one path before you reach your destination.'

'Thank you,' said Mawgan. 'We will be more diligent in our observations of the compass in the future.'

'Which one of you wears it?' asked the Merwoman.

'The girl,' said another watery voice near Darcy. 'She has it.'

Darcy suddenly felt very conspicuous as all Mer-eyes turned in her direction. She was not entirely convinced that these eyes were at all friendly.

'It's ok, Darcy,' whispered Mawgan. 'They won't hurt you, not while you carry something as precious to them as a compass. They want it too.'

'Is that supposed to make me feel better?' Said Darcy, 'because it really doesn't.'

She felt very vulnerable. Her feet were cold. She looked down to see the green water lapping into her shoes. They were now standing on a diminishing sandbank; the tide was on the rise.

'Why do they want it?' said Darcy.

'They want to expand their territory,' said Mawgan. 'By travelling through to your world, they could do just that, Merfolk are very territorial, it's been a long time since they were in your world Darcy, and nothing would please them better than to put that right.'

'Mawgan,' said Kea. 'We need to go, the tide's comin' in.'

The water was now lapping around their ankles. Mawgan turned again and addressed the Merwoman.

'I understand that the possession of a compass would be pleasing to you.'

The Merwoman nodded.

'I wish to make a bargain. If you ensure our safe passage through these waters, I will ensure the compass is passed to you once Darcy here has gone through the door. I do not know how you will use it, but you have my word.'

'How we would use it is not your concern,' said the Merwoman. 'But we thank you and agree to your terms.'

The company quickly made their way back into the launch and rowed to the ship. Although the Merfolk left them alone, Darcy felt they were nearby, a sinister presence, hidden, yet not far away, always watching.

Back onboard the ship, she rechecked the compass.

'Still north East?' said Mawgan.

'Yes,' said Darcy.

He gave the captain a nod to continue their way. The huge mainsail billowed into life again as the night breeze caught it and they were underway. Darcy couldn't help looking over the side into the now inky blackness below. A silver flash just below the surface glistened in the moonlight for a second, then it was gone. All this time, Nix and Hicca had watched everything from up in the crow's nest. The Merfolk made them nervous, and Hicca breathed steadily again now the company was all safely back on-board ship.

'I don't mind tellin' 'ee Nix,' he said. 'I don't trust them, they'ree Merfolk, neva 'ave and neva will.'

Nix looked at him in agreement. From her position in the nest, she could see clearly into the water below. Under the bow of the ship, keeping pace perfectly was a large school of Merfolk. Their presence would be constant all through the long night.

As dawn broke, it happened. Darcy and Kea were deep in conversation about the virtues of river fishing over sea fishing.

'There's nothin' to sea fishin', `ee jus' sit aboard 'ee boat danglin' 'ee line and them fishes fair jump straight on 'ee hook,' said Kea. 'Now then, take river fishin', 'ee 'ave to be a lot more sneaky when catchin' river fish, they are jus' that bit smarter.'

Something made Darcy look down at the compass. She had an inexplicable urge to do so. As she watched it, the compass spun. Slowly at first, so slowly that it was hard to detect the movement, then faster and faster it went. Kea pointed.

'We'll blow me down,' he said. 'Look at tha' thing.'

Darcy glancing down at the now spinning compass cried out.

'Mawgan! I think you need to look at this.'

Mawgan rushed over to her.

'What do I do?' Darcy asked.

'Wait.' said Mawgan. 'Wait and watch.'

They were soon joined by the others, all staring intently at the spinning pointer. It began to slow; slower and slower it went until it finally came to a stop. East. Mawgan hailed the captain.

'You'd better make for the shore; this is as far as we go.'

The captain immediately shouted orders for the mainsail to be brought in, and the ship slowed as he ordered it to turn towards the land.

High up in the crow's nest, Nix and Hicca were very excited.

'Nix, what are they doing?' cried Hicca. 'What would make them put in 'ere for goodness sakes?'

Mawgan looking up saw them. Nix changed and floated down to the deck, down the gangway into the belly of the ship and off towards the captain's staterooms. Mawgan followed her. Once in the staterooms, she changed herself back.

''Ee can't put in 'ere Mawgan,' she said. 'It's not safe.'

Mawgan put a hand gently on her shoulder. Even wizards were wary of being too close and personal with magical creatures, but he could see she was anxious.

'We must,' he said. 'If we are to follow the compass, then we must go exactly where it leads us, no matter where and no matter how difficult or dangerous.'

Nix, calmer now, continued to repeat her concerns, but Mawgan was adamant. They were going ashore, and they were going ashore here.

On deck Darcy, Morwenna, Glewas and Kea watched the shoreline grow as the ship made its way closer. Mawgan eventually rejoined them, and Nix returned to Hicca in the crow's nest. A good way off from shore the boat came to a stop, and those crew on deck prepared the small launch to get them ashore. Once it was ready, everyone got in. Two lights left the crow's nest above and headed north up the shoreline.

'Where are they going?' asked Darcy.

'They will travel north and rejoin us when they can, they cannot follow where we are going,' Mawgan replied.

'Where's that?' she asked.

The bottom of the launch touched shingle. The crew jumped into the shallows to pull it up onto the beach. Mawgan looked about him warily as he climbed out of the boat.

'This is the land of the Fae,' he replied. Darcy was still confused as they made their way further up the beach and turned to wave off the launch as the crew headed back to the ship.

'The land of the Fae, or Faerie, I think you call it,' Morwenna said.

Darcy's mouth hung open. Morwenna raised her index finger under Darcy's chin and closed it for her.

'Welcome to Faerie Land,' she said.

CHAPTER EIGHT

THE LAND OF THE FAE

'Let's get off this beach, we're easy targets out here,' said Mawgan.

He passed Morwenna and Darcy. Glewas and Kea were already heading up towards a bank of dunes and some tree cover.

'I wouldn't worry,' Morwenna said to Morgan's back as he clambered up the dune. 'They'll already know we're here, probably did even before we decided to come ashore.'

Mawgan stopped, turned and nodded in agreement.

'That may well be true,' he said, 'but let's not make it too easy for them. Shall we?'

He gestured up towards the top of the dune and started climbing again.

'These Fae; the way you talk about them; they don't sound very friendly.' said Darcy.

'Friendly is not a word I would use to describe the Fae,' replied Morwenna. 'It's more like you're a toy, something for their amusement, and when they're done with you, you're discarded.'

'What you have to understand,' said Glewas as they caught up to him, 'is that the Fae are magic.'

'I understand that,' said Darcy.

'No, I don't think you do,' said Glewas. 'You see, wizards and witches, well, we can use magic through spells and incantations, people say we have the magic, but there is a big difference between having the magic and being magic. With the Fae, magic lives within them and around them. They don't have to conjure it, it's who they are, and they cannot be separated from it.'

Darcy thought about this for a moment. Eventually, she said. 'What do they look like?'

'They look like you and me,' said Morwenna.

'Or a tree, a flower, an animal,' said Glewas. 'When you are as powerful as the Fae, everything else appears to be a lesser thing, insignificant. That's how the Fae view the world and everything in it.'

They reached the top of the dunes and headed into the trees. An owl hooted in a branch overhead, followed a few seconds later by another, then another.

'Tha's a signal,' Kea said, 'owls don't hunt in the daytime. Everyone keep 'ee eyes peeled.'

The company continued to make their way through the wooded area. The air changed. It became thick, sickly, and stifling hot. Darcy coughed, she couldn't breathe, she had to forcefully suck in the air to get it down into her lungs. They felt like they were on fire. She was dizzy. Everything seemed to be getting darker, further away. The last thing she remembered before passing out was looking across to where Mawgan had been a few feet from her. He was now lying in a heap on the ground. She heard an irritating, high pitched buzzing in her ears, then there was nothing but blackness.

There was no way of knowing how much time had passed. Darcy slowly became aware of herself again. She was cold, the ground underneath her was damp, she realised she was sitting, leaning against something. She reached behind her, it felt rough, could it be bark? A tree? She was leaning against a tree. Everything was dark. It took her a few seconds to realise her eyes were still closed. Slowly she opened them, a millimetre, then another, allowing time to adjust and to focus. It wasn't dark, in fact, it was very bright. The sun was high, she could see it through the branches and leaves overhead, and it made her eyes water. Glewas stirred to her right and rubbed his head. To her left Kea, Mawgan and Morwenna were in various stages of wakefulness. They were not alone. Darcy's vision was clearing, she could see directly ahead of her now, approximately fifty feet from her position were two of what she could only assume to be Fae. They were speaking in hushed voices, and she couldn't make out what they were saying. She looked at them carefully. They were tall, male and lean, almost bordering on the waif-like. But one thing stood out above all, they were twins. They were identical in every way, images of each other, flawless and beautiful. She suddenly realised that during her observation, she had been holding her breath, she let it out now in a long, slow, constant stream. To her surprise, it came out as a little sigh. Glewas' hand was on her shoulder.

'Are you alright?' he said.

'Yes, I think so, but I don't think I can move my legs.'

'No, me neither. They feel like they're tied, but I can't see anything holding them.'

Darcy looked more closely at her legs stretched out on the grass in front of her. It was true. She couldn't see anything holding them, but it felt distinctly like a rope had been twisted around them. The more she tried to move, the tighter she felt the invisible rope become. Kea swiped at his legs in a desperate, feeble effort to free himself.

'Stop that Kea and calm down,' said Morwenna. 'It won't help anyway, you'll just end up hurting yourself.'

'I can't jus' sit 'ere doin' nothin'' Kea replied.

Mawgan decided enough was enough. Sitting as upright and dignified as the situation would allow, he addressed the Fae who were still talking a few feet away from them and had not been troubled in the least by the company's whinges and moans.

'Can you please tell me why we are being held here against our will?'

The two Fae continued their conversation, not even looking once in Mawgan's direction. Mawgan had another go.

'I said, please tell us why we are being held in this way?'

Both Fae looked across at Mawgan this time and answered him in perfect and complete unison.

'No, that's not what you said, you said "can you please tell me why we are being held against our will," if you're going to repeat a question, then at least have the presence of mind to actually repeat it.'

Mawgan made an impolite 'grumph' noise, which seemed to amuse the two Fae.

'Why are you here?' they said. 'These lands are Fae; you have no business being here.'

'We need passage across,' Mawgan replied. 'We would not have disturbed you, except there is no other way.'

The Fae speaking in precise unison said,

'Where is the pixie filth you travel with? We saw all seven of you leave the vessel, but only five have come to this place.'

This time it was Morwenna who responded.

'They are not with us, they are respectful of the treaty and would not violate it; they will find their way by other means.'

The two Fae nodded. Their movements, although apparently spontaneous, were so coordinated, they appeared to be choreographed like an intricate dance. With a flick of their right wrists, the invisible bindings around the legs of the company disappeared. Darcy, Kea, Glewas, Morwenna, and finally Mawgan scrambled to their feet.

'Follow us,' said the Fae.

Without discussion or any objection, they all did.

Darcy wondered to herself why she had so readily agreed to go with the Fae. Not one of the company had said a word against it; they had all got to their feet and plodded on behind them like faithful dogs following their masters or mistresses. Darcy realised she was just beginning to understand what Glewas had said about the power the Fae had over everything around them. They could control and manipulate, to attempt to resist was futile.

'Why are we doing this?' Darcy asked Mawgan.

He was just ahead of her.

'There would be little point in not complying,' he said. 'The Fae could make us follow them. In fact, I think they are doing just that. Have you noticed how at this moment you are not inclined to do anything else?'

'Yes,' said Darcy, 'I really want to recheck the compass, but I don't seem to have the strength in my mind to focus on it.'

'Just as well,' Mawgan said, his voice barely a whisper. 'If we can keep it from them, it would be wise.'

Darcy's hand automatically went to the compass around her neck. Tucked down and secreted in her clothing, it was well hidden, and she made a fervent wish that it would remain that way.

From her position just behind Mawgan, Darcy could see the strange, lumbering mass she assumed was Kea. He seemed to be undergoing some peculiar internal struggle. A few feet further they edged their way into a small clearing. The light rose slightly, and Darcy could see clearly now Kea's struggling. He appeared to be having problems with the coordination of his legs. He was trying to get them to move him in a different direction, but no matter how hard he tried, digging his heels into the dirt, pushing and pulling at them, even bending over at one point and wrapping his arms around them, trying to hold them still, on they went, one in front of the other.

'Give it up, Kea,' Glewas moaned. 'It's useless to fight it, you'll just wear yourself out, and even then, they will still make you walk.'

'Aaaar!' Kea blurted in frustration. 'Where are we goin' anyway?'

'To meet someone who will decide what to do with us, I imagine,' said Glewas. 'These two don't look that important, just scouts I would think. We'll be off to see some head person, so you'll need to be on your best behaviour if we're ever going to get out of here.'

'Glewas is right, Kea,' said Morwenna, bringing up the rear of the walking party. 'Just keep going, the sooner we get to wherever they're taking us, the better. I want this over and done with as soon as possible; this place really gives me the creeps.'

They walked on, mostly in silence, following the two Fae much like the stolen children in the story of the Piper of Hamlin, only this time there was no piper to motivate them along, just two silent figures striding out in front and an unrelenting, inexplicable urge to move after them.

'Are you alright, Darcy?' Glewas asked.

She twisted the top half of her body around as far as she could to look at him. His face was all concern and something else she couldn't quite put her finger on.

'Yes, I think so,' she said. 'I can't seem to focus properly on anything.'

'Just keep talking to me,' he said, 'it will help.'

She saw a flicker of what she thought to be emotion move in the deaths of his eyes for a brief second, then it was gone.

'If we ever make it to your gate, will you really go back through?' he asked.

She looked at him, puzzled. Of course, she would go through, how could she not? Her parents, her life—it was all on the other side of the gate. Why was he even asking her this? He shouldn't be asking her this, how dare he be asking her this. After everything they had risked, all of them, the constant danger. Anger grew in the pit of her stomach. She felt its spark ignite and grow within her until it found its way onto her face. Glewas dropped his eyes away and concentrated on his moving feet. He couldn't look at her and Darcy turned back, too angry to answer.

It started to rain. Large cold drops splatted through the branches overhead and ran down their clothes and their necks. Increasing their walking speed, the intention was to reach their destination quicker, but without knowing how far away that destination might be, there seemed to be little point to it. Just as Darcy was thinking to herself that she couldn't possibly get any wetter, when there it was, sparkling like glass against the now drab grey sky. It was a palace, one that was the stuff of dreams and tall tales. Darcy heard Kea actually suck in his breath. They were still a mile or so off, but the palace was enormous. Its turreted roofline soared upwards into the low rain clouds, so it was impossible to know for sure just how high it was. The construction material could reflect its surroundings. As they walked, it seemed to become invisible then visible again, one moment there, the next it had vanished. The strangeness of the building occupied their attention for the last part of the journey until, sooner than expected, they were at the gates. Towering intricate as a spider's web yet solid as a stone wall. The steel creatures that covered the vine–like surfaces moved up and down along its metal tendrils, pulling scary faces at each other and anyone else who happened to be around.

'Are they gargoyles?' asked Kea.

'No,' said Darcy. 'They're grotesques, gargoyles have waterspouts.'

A particularly ugly grotesque leaned in low over Kea's head and blew an enormous raspberry, sticking out his tongue and spraying Kea in small metal droplets of spit that pinged off the top of his head.

'Ouch! You little bugger.'

Kea raised his fist and shook it in the grotesques face. The little monster just turned away and continued its climb along the metal branch, its job satisfactorily concluded.

The gates heaved into action without warning, slowly turning inwards on enormous hinges until they had parted enough to reveal a pathway beyond. When the gates had fully opened, the two Fae moved on through without so much as a word of instruction to the rest of the company. The five friends stood exchanging wary looks with each other for the briefest moment before their legs propelled them forward again, through the gates and onto the pathway beyond. As they walked, the pathway glistened beneath their feet as if it were wet, but the rain that had been falling only minutes before had all but dried up, and the sun was again beating down on their heads. The path was as dry as a bone, and so it was that Darcy stared at it, wondering what would make it shimmer like that. Like a long narrow snake stretching out before her, the paved, sparkling surface appeared to have a life of its own, and she found it so disorientating, that she stumbled and quickly looked away, if only to make staying upright a more realistic prospect.

Keeping her gaze directly ahead, Darcy focussed her attention on the small of Glewas' back as he too stumbled along just ahead of her. What had he meant earlier when he had asked if she would go back home? It was such a strange thing to say. Wasn't this the whole point of what they were doing right now? They had to keep the compass far away from Narcasta, and they had to find a way for her to get home. Home. She had hardly thought of it for days now. The journey had taken all her mental energy and focus, but now as she stumbled along in line towards goodness knows what. Darcy experienced a wave of sickness that unravelled itself in the pit of her stomach and spread nauseating fingers up into her chest and throat until she thought she was going to choke with the intensity of it.

'So, this is what it's like to be homesick,' Darcy thought to herself.

She didn't know how to deal with the feeling, so hard as it was, she pushed it down and contained it. She would deal with it later, much later. She forced herself back to the present. They were entering a smallish courtyard through an arched stone doorway. Directly opposite was another doorway. Through this, they were into the impenetrable darkness of some room.

Darcy knew it must be a room because as she walked across its hard floor surface, she could hear her own footsteps along with those of the others echoing back at her off walls that were hidden from them in the blackness. Sensing some sort of object ahead of her, she stretched out her arms. Her hand scraped along a damp chilly surface as her legs moved her to the side and changed direction of their own accord. Up some stairs, along a narrow corridor and through another room until they stopped, dead centre in a cavernous chamber. The vaulted ceiling soared above them, tiny puffs of cloud scudding across from one side to another then back again, looking more closely, Darcy could see that there was a whole ecosystem living in the ceiling space, birds flew, weaving in and out of clouds as they passed. There was a loud splat next to her.

'Oh, yuck!' Kea said.

He wiped a hand over the top of his head to rid himself of bird poop.

'Could this get any worse?'

'Yes, it could,' said Mawgan.

His face was as white as ash, his eyes black and full. Fear. Kea visibly recoiled, sulking.

Little spots of water dribbled down from the scudding clouds above, Kea sighed. Darcy lifted her eyes to the ceiling. The clouds, white and fluffy only moments before, were now dark and growing an increasingly ugly grey colour. A bolt of electricity shot from one cloud and hit a bird hard in the head; it fell, instantly dead, a crumpled black heap smoking on the floor. There was a crack appearing in the ceiling, minuscule, but it was defiantly there. Darcy screwed up her eyes as she concentrated on it. The crack widened, making a sound like splitting wood as it did so. They were all looking at it now. Kea's mouth drooping open as he stared, Mawgan looked like he was going to throw up.

The rest of them just kept looking up, motionless, drawn to keep on looking, no matter what was to happen next. The darkness intensified, the clouds whirling now, forming a perfect miniature storm in the roof space, just beneath the ever more menacing crack; it was a good foot in width now and growing bigger by the second. The shaking of the walls in the room brought everyone's concentration back to each other.

'It's an earthquake,' Morwenna shouted. 'Everyone hold on.'

The beautiful plasterwork that had ornately covered the walls only moments before was now falling in great clumps, crashing onto the floor and causing puffs of dust to form in the air. Breathing was becoming increasingly more difficult, and everyone broke out into fits of coughing, bending over with hands covering their mouths and wiping away tears from their eyes. In all the commotion, they had failed to notice that someone else had entered the room. He clapped his hands, and the shaking ceased. The crack in the ceiling healed itself immediately, and the plaster magically made its way back up the walls into place. The once stormy clouds reformed again into little white puffs, and all was as before.

'My house doesn't seem to like you. Why is that I wonder?'

The plaster dust mist that had shrouded them minutes before cleared to reveal the Lord of the Fae.

Cadan was impressive. At nearly seven feet tall, with hair the colour of raven feathers and broadness through the shoulders and back that spoke of a powerful body beneath sleek, well-tailored robes. He had eyes of a deep sapphire blue, a chiselled jawline and high cheekbones. They all looked on at the vision before them, mesmerised, but not by magic. It was the sheer spectacle of him that kept their attention.

'We were forced to come here. If the house doesn't like it, then there wasn't much to be done,' said Mawgan.

Cadan smiled. 'Yes, it must appear that way, but you have magic Mawgan. Yet you chose not to use it. In this instance, I find that a bit strange.'

'I know when I'm beaten,' said Mawgan. 'There would have been little point to fight it.'

Again, the smile crept slowly across Cadan's face. It had the effect of making him appear slightly less formidable, and the atmosphere in the room noticeably warmed.

'So,' Cadan said.

His face suddenly hardened, and the room cooled again.

'Why are you all here? And why is it you smell of pixies?'

His nose crinkled in disgust at what he obviously found to be a terrible smell.

'We are here because we have little choice,' said Morwenna.

There was a strange tone in her voice. Darcy could not place it, but she was reminded of something, she just couldn't remember what at that moment. Kea shuffled his feet. He had been very subdued since Cadan had entered the room, and now he stood huddled, his head hanging.

'What's up with you?' Darcy asked.

He raised his head slightly and looked at her out of the corner of his eye before replying.

'I don' like Fae, they're sneaky blighters, don' trust a word out of his mouth.'

Darcy nodded and listened again to Morwenna. There it was, just like before, that tone in her voice. What was that?

'Oh, my god!'

Everyone in the room turned to look at her. Darcy, realising that she had said that out loud, took a step back and looked at the floor. After a few more seconds, noting that nothing was wrong, Morwenna and Cadan continued their conversation, this time though Darcy wasn't listening; she had it, that tone in Morwenna's voice. She knew what it was, and she was blown away by it. Morwenna loved Cadan. That thought kind of disgusted her. She didn't know how anyone could be in love with a person so manipulative and controlling—well she was only fourteen years old after all—Darcy hadn't really had any experience of any kind of relationship other than that with her parents and a few scattered friendships here and there. Something was going on between herself and Glewas. She felt it when she was with him. Still, romantic love was an experience yet to come in her life, but Darcy was knowledgeable enough to recognise it in others when she saw it, and she was seeing it now.

CHAPTER NINE

CADAN AND MORWENNA

A number of years before...

It was dark. The kind of darkness where you can't see your hand, even if you hold it up and wiggle your fingers right in front of your eyes. Morwenna wiggled her fingers like mad, but no, she couldn't see a thing. She reached down to her right leg, which she suddenly realised was throbbing in pain. Her brain had blocked this sensation until now, but with the action of touching the leg had come to the realisation and the awareness that something was very wrong with it. Reaching up now, she felt her head, something wet and slightly sticky smeared over her fingers. She sniffed at them, now just under her nose and smelt the unmistakable metallic whiff of blood. She knew instantly it was her blood. Tears stung the back of her eyes. Frustrated, as she didn't think she was crying, she sniffed them back. She was lying on the ground, and as she couldn't be sure if or when the men with the dogs would be back, she knew she had to move away from there and find some shelter, somewhere Morwenna could hide and protect herself until she had figured out what to do next. Morwenna pressed her hands into the dirt to give some leverage to her efforts to stand; it was then she felt the wetness on the ground and knew it was more of her blood. Pushing as hard as she could, she tried to get to her feet. Very slowly, and with maximum effort, she stood. Her right leg would not support any weight, so she limped a few steps, dragging the almost useless leg along until she smacked into a tree and stood hugging it for support, her breath coming in heavy gasps with the effort. Now she really was crying, a combination of pain, frustration and the feeling of being alone, completely alone.

Morwenna realised she could now see the outline of her fingers on the trunk of the tree she was holding, then she realised she saw the tree too. There was a glow around her.

'It must be morning,' she thought.

But then, thinking again, concluded that this was not the dawn, it was green for a start. The light was behind her. Ever so slowly she started, stiffly, to turn herself around. It was difficult with a useless leg and took a lot longer than it would have usually taken her. There, a few feet from where she stood, were two full size pixies. She looked at them for a second, then she fainted.

Hicca got to Morwenna in time to stop her from flopping onto the ground. 'Ere Nix, she's hur' badly like,' he said.

He scooped Morwenna up into his arms. At seventeen, she was full grown but still had the slightness of girlhood about her and was not heavy at all to him. Nix put a hand on Morwenna's forehead.

'Oooh, she's burnin' up Hicca, she'll not last long without propa care, bu' where are we gonna take her?'

'I 'ave no idea Nix my lover, bu' I do knows one thing, we can' stay 'ere. We 'ave ta move, them there dog's 'll be back 'n' 'ee knows 'ow much I hate them dogs.'

They moved, walking at a speed only magical folk can manage they cleared the woods and were now into the vast swathes of farmland surrounding that part of Dumnonia.

'Dawns a-comin',' Nix pointed to the east.

Sure enough, the very first glimpses of light crept onto the horizon.

'Dam 'n' blast,' said Hicca. 'We'll be seen, we can't be seen, they'll kill 'er next time they find 'er.'

'The only way is t' fly Hicca. We'll 'ave t' fly 'er out of 'ere, we need t' get 'er somewhere safe.'

'Where's tha'?' said Hicca. 'There's nowhere safe in these parts.'

'I know,' said Nix.

She rubbed her head for a moment, straining with the effort of thinking. Then it came to her, a flicker of certainty at first spread over her face, then the confidence of her smile.

'Home Hicca. We're takin' 'er home.'

They flew all day, Morwenna woke for a few minutes but she was delirious with fever, muttered a few nonsensical words and nothing more. They flew all the next night, their burden passed between them at intervals to let the other rest. Then it was morning again, and as the dawn grew, they approached the outskirts of the Vale.

Flying through the Vale is like flying with your face to the sun. Before you enter, everything is ordinary, nothing suspicious, or different enough to provoke a question in your mind. Then it's upon you, the blinding, suffocating light that burns your eyeballs, it's like acid on your skin. For anyone not pixie it would be terrifying, but for Nix and Hicca, it was the welcoming light of home. They passed through with ease, not affected by it in the least. They were concerned at first how Morwenna would go passing through, but their concern was unnecessary. She was unconscious still and while she was in their care; she was unaffected by it. Once through the barrier the pixie homelands stretched out before them, a vast patchwork of flower fields—pixies are flower eaters, they will occasionally eat fruit or vegetables but definitely no meat—and homes, very similar to those lived in by humans in Dumnonia, cottages, farmhouses and outbuildings. Thatched and tiled roofs sped past, and Nix turned her head to look at Hicca.

'Home at last' she said.

They both gratefully landed and took their human-like form.

Morwenna woke in a sea of cotton, feather pillows and eiderdown. As the sleepy fog in her brain cleared, she realised she was in a pretty bedroom. Sunlight lit the bright cotton fabrics and wooden furniture around the room. She didn't know how she had gotten there or even where 'there' was, but she was aware of a sensation of complete and total peacefulness. Her right leg was bandaged, she could tell from the absence of any pain that it was healing. Touching her head, her fingers traced the fine line of a scar where she had felt the sticky blood the night before. Was it the night before? She realised that she could not tell how much time had passed. Her brain understood logic would dictate a time-lapse of more than just one night, given the condition of her injuries and how much they had already healed. How long had it been? Three or four days at least, and where on earth was she? This was nothing like her bedroom at home, and where were all her books? Swinging her legs carefully out of bed, Morwenna slowly made her way over to the window and drew back the white cotton drapes. She smiled to herself at the little pink rosebuds sprayed here and there about them that caught the light as they moved. Peering outside, she could see the front of the house. A small path wound its way to a garden gate, on either side were planted herbs and flowers, the window was slightly ajar, and the smell wafted in towards her, sage, parsley and there was rosemary thickly planted by the gate.

'For protection?' she smiled.

These people, whoever they were, knew their herbs. The wind caught the leaves and scent of a Rowan tree in the centre of a carefully tended lawn, as the tangy smell wafted into her, for the first time in many years, Morwenna knew what it felt like to be completely and utterly safe. She liked it.

Before long, Morwenna understood everything that had happened as told to her by Nix and Hicca, and so it was that she came to be the unlikely adopted witch daughter of two very precocious pixies. Morwenna thrived. She honed her craft; being always surrounded by magic made this more straightforward than it had ever been before, and she grew into her powers. A Hedge Witch, healer. For four years she practised until, as her twenty-first birthday approached, she knew it was time, and she was ready.

Trying to explain her plans to Nix and Hicca without Hicca bursting into fits of uncontrollable crying was impossible, but the alternative of staying put was not an option in Morwenna's mind. She was determined to leave and take up her rightful place in the village she had so cruelly been exiled from four years before and face the people who had driven her away.

'I'm ready for this, and I need to do it.'

She explained this across the dinner table one evening. Both Hicca and Nix could see her determination, and so, even though they were heartbroken, they did what every parent of a grownup child must eventually do, they waved her off, with their blessing and their love, and hoped that they had given her enough.

Skip forward three years...

The night of Yule, the midwinter festival. Morwenna was in the woods gathering holly for garlands and as much Feverfew and Willow Bark as she could get her hands on to brew her tea for headache relief. Always very popular at this time of year. She had built herself a life in Piddleton Village. She was tolerated because she was useful. The other villagers overlooked who Morwenna was in favour of her healing practice, and so they all rubbed along in a hostile peace. She belonged to, but never really was a part of village life. Nix and Hicca would visit from time to time, but for the most part, her existence was a solitary one.

Morwenna knew that there was a large crop of Feverfew to be found at the edge of Willow Wood. She had spotted the daisy-like flowers earlier that summer and hoped that the frost hadn't ended them entirely for the year. Sure enough, as she approached the spot, she saw the tiny white heads and the bright yellow centres of the flowers still poking through the hard frost and hurried to them. She was so engrossed in her collecting that she had not heard the footsteps of someone approaching.

'What are you doing?'

Morwenna looked up, startled, and saw a man, very tall, very dark like her, dressed for travel. Thinking to herself that he didn't look like he would pose a threat, she continued picking the plants.

'Collecting Feverfew, it's good for a hangover headache.'

'Yes,' he said. 'Among other things. You should try it on old George's arthritis.'

'You know George, do you?' she said.

Morwenna stopped picking and looked up. He was gone.

The next day, she was swamped. George, Bill and Harry visited her for the hangover tea, just as she knew they would. Harry had thrown up all over her doorstep, very much still drunk from the night before. Other villagers too had come and asked her for help in dealing with the excesses of the season, and as always, she had obliged them with her usual, non-judgmental, doctoring, handing out relief in various medicinal forms. Morwenna had told George to keep taking the tea as it may help with his arthritis and that she would be interested in finding out how he found it. He had left, promising to return and let her know, but she was doubtful he would. He usually avoided her like a wort, unless he needed something. She would ask him the next time he visited. Whenever that would be.

Morwenna knelt, scrubbing brush in one hand, a bucket of soapy water in the other, trying to clean the step of whatever Harry had eaten and drunk the night before.

'Yuck, this really is disgusting.'

'Looks it,' he said.

He was back.

'Hello,' said Morwenna.

The thought entered her head that he must believe she was only four feet tall, given that she was on her knees again. Morwenna stood and brushed down her skirts.

'What can I do for you?' She asked.

Ready to fill another prescription.

'Oh, I'm just passing. Did you have a good Yule?'

His question seemed a little odd to Morwenna given what she was doing, but she answered anyway.

'I don't celebrate it, there doesn't seem to be much point when you're on your own. Yule is a festival for families and friends to share, I don't have any, really.'

She didn't know why she had said that. She shrugged and knelt again to scrub the step, pulling a disgusted face. He clicked his fingers. She heard the sharp little click, and the vomit was gone. It vanished, along with her brush and bucket of water. She found the whole thing a bit annoying.

'Fancy a drink?' he said.

Morwenna was getting to her feet again. He held out a bottle of beer to her.

'Where's my brush and bucket?'

'Away.'

He walked on past her and into the house. He walked down the hall into the kitchen and opened a thin cupboard door, a broom cupboard, and there was the bucket and brush. Away.

'See,' he said.

Morwenna walked up behind him. She didn't know what to feel first, gratitude that he had cleaned up for her, or anger that he had just walked into her home uninvited and seemed to know his way around. She ended up reaching for the bottle of beer in his hand, taking a considerable swig before saying.

'Yeah, I see.'

They talked. Morwenna was surprised when the sun peeped through the curtains announcing that a new day had arrived. Spending time with him felt like putting on an old forgotten piece of clothing, a favourite, suddenly found again from the recesses of your wardrobe. Putting it on, you feel the comfort of something familiar yet newly discovered.

'I must go,' he said.

'Ok,' said Morwenna. 'Will you be back?'

He winked at her and vanished.

Six months later to the day, Morwenna woke an hour before dawn and prepared to leave the house. The wheel of the year had turned a full half, today was the 21st June, the festival of Litha, she walked across the village square, each home and building was festooned in flowers from pub door to church steeple. She joined the rear of a procession of villagers making their way by torchlight to the stones. They were going to wait for the sun, to mark the passing of the seasons as they had done for centuries past and would do for those yet to come. The midsummer solstice was here.

The moor looked unreal in the light from the torches and the waning moon. The very first dim touches of the promised sun were lighting the eastern corners of the horizon. Morwenna pulled back from the procession. She knew her presence on such a morning would make the villagers nervous, so she was planning on staying out of the stone circles. She took up position by the Piper stones, not realising that there were three stones this morning, not the usual two that stood separate to the others on the moor. She would watch the proceedings from there. It was cold even though it was summer, and she pulled her cloak tight around her.

'Chilly?' Enquired the stone next to her.

Morwenna jumped back, startled.

'Oh! It's you,' she said.

It was light enough now to see the smile on his face. He could look scary, but at that moment, she was reminded of a cheeky little boy. She returned his smile and relaxed.

'How did you do that?' she asked.

'Don't you know the stories of the stones?' he said.

'No. What stories? Shall we stop answering each other with a question?'

He laughed.

'There are those who believe that the stones are really men, frozen for all time because of something they did, but no one now remembers who they were, or what they were supposed to have done, they remember only that these were men and now they are stones.'

'Do you know what happened to them?' said Morwenna.

'I was told the story as a child. It was a very different time. Humans, fae, and pixies fought each other for the lands around the moor and Tintagel. It is said that those who hold the castle hold the entire region, and so it was then too. Amid all the battles between the three peoples was a rumour, a whisper of a power not yet seen in these parts, not yet known but coming. The fae and pixies were so busy killing each other to notice the slow sickness of complacency that was spreading amongst the humans. They had no appetite for fighting anymore when they were threatened, they just ran away, gave up, moved on. So it was that Narcasta crept onto the land and into the minds of the people without anyone really noticing. Like a slow-working poison, paralysing the body inch by inch until it is too late to be saved, he moved through the land spreading his brand of darkness as he went until there were no safe places left for good people to hide. One Sunday morning, a couple of travelling musicians came to the castle. They would often play for food and shelter and approached the kitchen gate with the intention of applying to the housekeeper for some breakfast. One had a fiddle, the other a pipe, and they played the sweetest music, full of happiness and the promise of better days. The housekeeper and kitchen maids felt their hearts lighten at the sound. It pushed away the darkness for a moment and made them forget how hard their lives were for a time. Narcasta heard the music too. He realised its power, and he was afraid. He made his way down to the kitchens and found the musicians there eating. He invited them to walk with him, and taking the instruments along with them, they had played their happy tunes until they reached Bodmin. With a flick of his hand, Narcasta turned them into stones on the moor, forever to endure their punishment and be a warning to others not to bring light into a place where darkness was the only power.'

'Narcasta's hold on us is fading,' said Morwenna. 'Look.'

She pointed, turning to the east. The sun was rising. Even though Morwenna had seen the sunrise on every midsummer morning since she was a girl, it never failed to impress her with its beauty. As the rays of the sun reached the surfaces of the stones, he walked up to her, took her face in his hands and kissed her, and they were engulfed in the light.

A month later, as she was leaving Nix and Hicca at the garden gate of their home, she could hear Nix calling after her.

'Be safe, my lovely.'

The warm, fuzzy feeling of being well-loved made Morwenna smile to herself. During her visit, she had tried several times to broach the subject of her stranger with Nix and Hicca, but the moment was never right, and so she was leaving without sharing her news. Over years of visits and quite a few near misses when it came to Morwenna entering and exiting the Vale, the Pixies had devised a way for her to come and go unaffected by it. She knew better than to ask how it was done. It was done for her, and she was grateful for it. That was all that was needed. The fact that she could visit her adoptive pixie parents whenever she wanted to, and they could visit her sustained her, and the loneliness she endured lessened slightly. Although a witch, Morwenna's craft was more a healing art, she had none of the more spectacular skills, she couldn't fly, her besom was good for sweeping the front step and that was all. She didn't have the talent for turning unsuspecting folk into inanimate objects or lower-order creatures. No matter how much she sometimes longed to have that skill. So it was that travelling home from a visit without the help of Nix and Hicca meant a long walk, a weeklong journey. That's what Morwenna would have had ahead of her now, but for the fact that she had booked a passage on the boat down the coast. That would speed things up a little, and so she made her way to the harbour.

Morwenna lazed most of the day of the passage away on deck. The sun was warm on her face, and she was happy. There was the most awful crunching sound. The noise was sudden, and obviously unexpected by the crew. The ship shuddered and came to a complete and not very graceful stop. The sailors ran about the deck in flurries of disorganised concern.

'It's the mainsail,' called the captain. 'The mast, make haste, clear the deck, she's going to go.'

The crew herded the passengers into a launch, lowered it onto the sea and rowed a little way from the ship. Morwenna could see the mast precariously teetering first one way, then the other, before toppling over entirely and splashing into the waves.

'That'll never do,' said a sailor.

'Ere' do ya know where we've landed up?' said another.

'Shhh,' the first sailor said. 'No point scaring 'em.'

Pointing forward towards the passengers.

'They'll know soon enough.'

Morwenna steeled herself, but for what she didn't know. They were soon at the shoreline and ran to get out of the sun. It seemed much hotter on the beach than it had been on the water. They climbed the dunes to a line of trees just above them.

Morwenna was awake, but she didn't know from what. She had no recollection of falling asleep, but she felt like she had been.

'Where was she?'

She didn't have an answer, so decided the best thing would be to take account of her surroundings. She was propped up on a chaise, pillows behind her, and a soft, light blanket covered her legs. Yes, good. That was a start. She looked about the room, yes it was a room, huge with ornate plasterwork covering the walls, the walls themselves were covered 360 degrees by an idyllic country scene. Morwenna looked up, clouds scurried from one side of the roof space to the other, birds called to each other across the void and circled in play, glad to just be alive and able to fly. Someone took her hand, and she was brought sharply back to ground level. He was kneeling next to her, his face concerned but not overly so.

'You look better,' he said.

Still holding her hand. She snatched it back in surprise.

'Oh,' she said.

Then her mouth had finally reconnected to her brain.

'Where are we?' she said.

'You are in my home, my guest. Now, is there anything you need?'

He smoothed a stray hair across her forehead with the tip of his index finger. The feel of it seemed to burn a path across her brow; his hand tingled as he removed the finger from her skin. He frowned as he got to his feet and held out his hand for her to follow him.

'Come on, I'll show you around.'

'Who are you?' said Morwenna.

He had shown her the house. They had talked and laughed at his explanations of things around the place, his interpretation of the building's external, shiny, glass-like appearance had made her giggle when he told her it, 'Fooled the birds that were forever trying to land and poop all over it.'

They had eaten a meal consisting of good roasted lamb with all the trimmings and a nice bottle of some wine that tasted of summer and made her head spin slightly. It also left a warm glow on her cheeks. He looked at her as she sat opposite him. She was searching his face for any sign of a hint of the answer to her question, but he was as inscrutable as always.

'Ah,' he said, 'so we come to it then. Well, I knew we would have to at some point, but I'm afraid it will change everything.'

'You, afraid?' she said. 'That's unlikely. I don't think I've ever met anyone less likely to be afraid in my life.'

She considered him for a moment. He was magical. She already knew that. The bucket disappearing act had cemented that fact for her after their second meeting, but it was more than that. He didn't conjure. No incantations were chanted to remove the bucket and brush from the step and from out of her hand.

'So,' she said. 'You're magical.?'

It was a statement really, not a question. He nodded his answer, and she continued.

'Not a pixie?'

'No,' he said. 'Definitely not Pixie.'

The look on his face was disgusted at her suggestion, and in that very moment, she had it.

The thought started as a single disturbance in her brain, a remembrance of something long forgotten. Her mind reached for the recollection and eventually it came to her, the emotion of the comprehension spread over her face until her disgust mirrored his.

'You're Fae,' she said.

Morwenna got to her feet, carefully pushed her chair under the table, and left the room.

Ever since she was a little girl, Morwenna had heard the stories about the Fae people. A child goes missing. The Fae must have taken them. The harvest failed. The Fae were the ones to blame. Narcasta took control of Dumnonia, and the Fae were responsible. Then, she had gone to live with Nix and Hicca, and her view of the Fae became more than just merely clouded by superstition and prejudice. It was now seeded with hate. The Pixie peoples and the Fae had fought battles and wars since the people of Dumnonia had kept records of such things. The last hundred years though had seen a strained truce between them, each side keeping to strict rules of conduct and separate areas of occupation. If they met on the road or in a village, they avoided more than the briefest of interactions or contact and went their separate ways as quickly as possible. Morwenna, being an adopted pixie, soon learned to share her family's viewpoint of the Fae situation. So her response to finding out that the man she was falling in love with was also a faerie, was never going to be a happy one.

Following her from the room, confused and worried, he called after her.

'What's wrong? I know my dinner conversation can leave a lot to be desired, but I didn't think it was that bad.'

Morwenna didn't turn around or stop walking, she made it to another door and walked right on through, only to come face to face with two more Fae. These were at least as tall, if not taller than he was.

'Lord Cadan,' they said in unison. 'Do you require assistance?'

'No,' said Cadan. 'Let her pass, she is free to go wherever she chooses.'

Now Morwenna did turn to face him.

'Lord Cadan?' She repeated.

She walked on past the two guards, making a line for the door on the wall opposite. She believed it led to a passageway he had shown her earlier to the outside.

'Morwenna.'

Cadan's voice was sincere and full of emotion. She found that it annoyingly made her body tingle. She once again turned to face him, and he was all of a sudden, a lot closer to her than she had expected. She flinched a little, stepping backwards at the same time.

'What's wrong?' he asked.

Cadan took hold of her trembling hand. She looked down at her feet, trying unsuccessfully to get her thoughts into some sort of order.

'I-er-you're, I mean, you are.'

'Faerie?' He finished the sentence for her.

'Yes, Faerie.'

As she said the words, he was looking right into her eyes, trying to read her.

'Is that a problem for you?'

His question wasn't an unreasonable one.

'You don't understand,' she said. 'It's not just who, or what you are, it's who I am too.'

'You're right,' said Cadan. 'I don't understand.'

Morwenna swallowed hard and took a deep breath.

'I'm human, but I'm also—er—Pixie.'

He stepped back, dropping her hand between them. He vanished.

The whole world started to shake. It began with the floor and got steadily worse until she couldn't keep her feet and fell over. Plaster fell around her, smashing down. The walls were undulating like a wave. There was the most tremendous noise. Any moment she imagined a steam train was going to charge through the place. Morwenna screamed. She rolled herself into the foetal position with her hands over the back of her head; her face buried between her knees and her eyes closed tight against the dust. She willed herself out of the room. If ever there was a time for her to find she had the ability to fly, this was it. But no, she was still on the floor. A massive piece of plaster from the ceiling crashed down, just missing her by a centimetre.

Morwenna was not really the fainting type, but the adrenaline in her body was playing havoc with her, and she was close, very close to losing consciousness. At a total loss as to what to do, pure panic and frustration drove her to yell at the top of her voice.

'Just bloody well stop it!'

Silence.

Where seconds before there had been total mayhem, now nothing, not the smallest of sounds were heard outside of her own body. Morwenna, however, could hear her heart pounding, fit to burst right out of her chest with the effort. She opened her eyes and uncoiled her body until she could sit. Looking around her, everything was as before; there was no sign of the destruction of a few moments ago. She wondered if she had imagined the whole thing?

'No.'

She pushed her middle finger into the soft part of her wrist. Her racing pulse was evidence of what had happened, even if nothing else was still visible.

'How did you manage that?'

Cadan was behind her. She spun around on her knees and stood, even though her legs were shaking like two jellies.

'I've never seen anyone control the house before,' he said. 'You obviously have more magic than you think Morwenna.'

She just looked at him, not sure if she trusted herself to say anything at that moment.

'I think we have things to discuss. Don't you?'

He took her hand once again and led her back, past the two Fae guards and into the dining room, pulling out a chair for her before returning to his own seat.

'You just left me.' said Morwenna.

'I know, I'm sorry,' he said. 'What you said though took me by surprise, I wasn't prepared for you—for you being Pixie.'

'No,' she said. 'Nor I, you being Fae. So, what are we going to do now?'

It was a valid question, but they both looked at each other, neither of them with an answer. It was impossible, they both knew it, and their sadness overwhelmed them. Neither could find a solution that enabled them to be together. So, they both resigned themselves to the solution of being apart.

She left later that same day, re-joining the rest of the ship's passengers on the beach, none of them was the worse for the experience of sleeping the day away—or so they thought—in the sunshine while the mainsail mast was repaired. They continued their journey down the coast just after sundown. Much later than they should have been, but on their way again, the mood was high, almost euphoric. The Merfolk sang them such beautiful songs. Morwenna was stirred to tears. She wasn't sure though if it was just the music or the hopelessness of her situation that was making her cry. The boat made its way slowly and surely to the southern harbour just as the sun rose and they began to disembark, bleary-eyed and weary. Morwenna had taken a concoction of her own making. A combination of Rhodiola Rosea mixed with Schizandra berries which had staved off the worst of her tiredness. She even felt a little lightheaded as she walked the last few miles towards home.

'It could be the combination of yesterday's wine, no sleep, and the drugs. Or, it could just be a combination of Cadan.'

She stopped herself thinking at that point. It was a useless situation anyway, there was no way it could be resolved, no way the outcome could be any different. She was Pixie. He was Faerie, that was the end of it.

For months afterwards, Morwenna carried on her life just as before. There was nothing external about her that would have indicated any change, but internally, everything had shifted. She was not the person she had been, nor would she ever be that person again. She longed for Cadan to turn up in her life, just as he had done in the past. Even though this was against everything she told herself she either needed or wanted; but he never showed. Morwenna would look for him when she was walking or collecting plants or was just out and about doing all the everyday stuff she always did. He never came to her. Morwenna began to doubt if she had ever loved him or him, her.

She had questioned their love until this moment.

Now, she stood across the room from him. He was looking at her and she at him. She felt a wave of emotion pushing at her heart. Her recently discovered friends were all around her, and then there was Darcy, the girl she had left everything to help and protect, looking up at her with the most curious expression on her face.

'Busted,' she said.

CHAPTER TEN

LITTLE VOICES

Darcy looked from Morwenna to Cadan and back again, and then she just looked at the ground, not really knowing where to put her eyes. She had stumbled across something sacred that wasn't for her. Darcy pretended she hadn't noticed.

'What do you want with us?' said Morwenna. 'We are no threat to you, you could have just given us passage through your lands and have done with it, but no, you had to interfere!'

She spoke with such force and conviction that Mawgan, Kea and Glewas were quite taken aback. Darcy, however, had understood Morwenna's motive. She was trying to throw her off the scent. Darcy was having none of it. To calm Morwenna down, she took her hand and held it. Morwenna's red rage left her face and her breathing slowed and became calm. She just looked at the floor. Cadan, who had not said a word during Morwenna's diatribe, spoke up.

'You all look as if you could manage something to eat.' Kea smiled. His stomach growled its approval. 'Let's retire to the dining room where a meal has been arranged. We can talk more comfortably about what's to happen next.'

The group made their way to the very next room, and sure enough, the table held a feast. Everyone's favourite foods were laid out.

''Ow did 'ee know?' Kea asked.

He tucked into whatever was in front of him as he drifted around the table.

'We are well versed in entertaining guests,' Cadan said. 'Let's sit. You will enjoy it so much better.'

The whole group found a seat and began to eat. Darcy chose a chair next to Morwenna, hoping to be able to have a chat about what she had seen happen in the hall without anyone else overhearing.

'So, what was that all about?' she asked.

Morwenna shrugged.

'Nothing I want to talk about.'

She carried on eating, not once looking at Darcy.

Darcy nudged at her elbow. Morwenna was forced to look at her.

'You two looked pretty intense in there. What's going on with you? You never told me you knew him. I mean, why would you? We're only friends, after all. Why would you say anything to me about it?'

Morwenna turned herself to face Darcy.

'You think I betrayed you,' she said. 'That I have something to hide.'

'Do you?'

Morwenna took a long, deep breath in and slowly released it.

'How can I possibly answer you in any way that would make you understand that I didn't betray you? That everything I have done so far has only ever been to help you.'

Darcy was young, but she wasn't a fool. She looked at Morwenna's eager face and knew she was telling her the truth.

'Darcy, it's not a simple thing, this situation, I wish it were. Cadan and I, we're just too different; the situation is hopeless. Nix and Hicca would never accept it.'

Darcy's mouth hung open.

'You mean to say they don't know about this?'

Morwenna flashed her a warning look. Darcy quickly closed her mouth and returned to munching on her dinner.

'No,' said Morwenna. 'They don't know. They won't understand.'

'I know I haven't had a long time to get to know Nix or Hicca,' said Darcy. 'But I don't think you're giving them much credit. If you explained...'

'No, Darcy. Just No.'

While Darcy and Morwenna were deep in conversation, neither of them noticed the chair on Darcy's other side move out, and someone sit next to her.

'So, Darcy, is it?' he said.

Darcy started. She swung around. Cadan stared. It made her nervous.

'Yes, that's right,' she said.

Cadan munched on a lettuce leaf. A tiny piece of it was visible peeping out of the corner of his mouth. Darcy had the overwhelming urge to laugh. It started as a giggle and bubbled up inside her until she thought her sides would burst with the effort of it.

'Stop it Cadan.' Morwenna frowned at him. 'That's not fair, leave her alone.'

'I was only trying to ease the tension,' he said. Morwenna shook her head in disapproval. 'So,' Cadan spoke to the whole group now. 'What am I to do with you all?'

'You could le' us go,' said Kea.

'Yes, I could,' said Cadan. 'But if I do, where will you disappear too next?'

His eyes narrowed. Cadan looked at each of them in turn. He eventually came to Morwenna. Now his eyes softened, and he smiled at her.

'Oh, for goodness' sake,' said Glewas.

'We need your help,' said Mawgan. 'We must move east, and He must not know about it.'

'By He, I assume you mean Narcasta?' said Cadan. 'That will be difficult, we try to keep these borders safe, as you know, but the Imps are often able to get through and keeping them blind to your presence may not be possible.'

'We must nevertheless risk it,' said Morgan. 'We are charged with a great task, the details of which I will not discuss, but we are committed and will see it through, whatever is to come.'

'I see,' said Cadan.

His eyes narrowed again.

'We have always trusted each other Mawgan, and even though you won't share with me this task that is so important to you, I trust to our friendship. We will help you as best we can. That is my promise to you. Maybe another time you can share with me what this is all about.'

'Another time,' said Mawgan.

They finished their meal and left the room. Darcy pulled Mawgan aside.

'Why didn't you tell him?' she asked. 'Surely if you trust him as you seem to do, it will only help if he knows why we are here.'

'Don't be fooled, Darcy,' said Mawgan. 'Cadan is not without his own agenda here. That is why I told you to keep the compass hidden. If he was to find out you had it, he would have no choice but to try and take it. He could not chance to leave it in the hands of one so young and inexperienced, and without it, you would have no chance of returning home.'

'I see,' said Darcy.

Her hand moved to the place beneath her neck where the compass was hidden. She hadn't dared look at it since they had been brought here, and now she wondered if she should have checked it to make sure they were still heading in the right direction.

'Don't,' said Mawgan. 'You mustn't risk it, not here, later when we are alone.'

Darcy nodded, and they followed the rest of the group.

Entering a large sitting room, the company noticed that it had been set up as a makeshift sleeping place with put up camp beds, enough for all of them, scattered around.

'They mean to keep us here indefinitely.'

Mawgan spoke softly to the back of Darcy's head.

'Sleep well,' said Cadan.

He smiled and winked at Darcy and Mawgan.

'We leave at dawn. Our eastern borders are a day's walk from here, so we will need an early start. Morwenna, Mawgan, I must speak with you before you rest, please join me in my chamber.'

Mawgan and Morwenna left the room with Cadan. Darcy, Kea and Glewas looked from one to the other.

'I wonder wha' tha' were all obou',' said Kea. 'It's way too much secretin' for me likin'.'

He shook his head.

'I agree,' said Glewas. 'There's definitely something going on. Did you see how Morwenna and Cadan kept looking at each other over dinner?'

'Oh, you two really are idiots sometimes,' said Darcy. 'They're in love, can't you see that?'

'Don' be so daft girl,' said Kea. 'He's Fae. She's 'alf Pixie. Tha's a recipe fer disaster if ever I 'eard o' one.'

'Well,' said Darcy. 'Disaster or not, it's happened. Maybe we should be trying to figure out how to help them.'

'Help them?' said Glewas. 'There will be no helping them if Nix and Hicca ever find out.'

'Righ' now,' said Kea, ''ee should be 'elpin' 'eeself by gettin' some rest befer mornin' arrives.'

Darcy and Glewas both nodded in agreement, and the three young friends settled for the remainder of the night. Just down the hall from them, though, things were very different.

'I've asked you to join me here because we need to discuss the Imps.'

Cadan had only just closed the door of the room behind them, but he wasted no time. There was none to waste.

'We know the Imps are a problem,' said Mawgan. 'But we have dealt with them before, we will do so again, I'm sure.'

Morwenna nodded in agreement.

'I heard about the last time you both had a run-in with the Imps,' said Cadan. 'Morwenna was nearly killed, I won't allow her to be hurt again.'

'Excuse me,' said Morwenna. 'It's nobody's business but my own, what I get myself involved in. It's my risk to take and no one else's.'

'Ok,' said Cadan. 'I can see your mind is made up. But everything is much worse than I gave the impression of. The Imps are all over our lands, searching and listening for word of you and most especially Darcy. I didn't want to discuss it in front of her.'

'Darcy is a lot stronger than you give her credit for,' said Morwenna. 'She's come up against the Imps before. She'll be fine, and we'll be there to look after her.'

Mawgan had been silent during this exchange between Morwenna and Cadan, but now he couldn't hold in his question any longer.

'The Imps have always been a problem since Narcasta brought them down from the north. Why are you now so concerned Cadan?'

Cadan looked at them both. His face was so pale at that moment. The blood had just drained away. Morwenna reached out and placed a hand on his arm. Cadan smiled again and patted her hand.

'Because now he knows things about what goes on here, which can only mean one thing.'

Mawgan's face went as pale as Cadan's.

'You have a traitor in your midst,' he said. 'I thought at least here we would be safe for a while.'

Mawgan's body seemed to shrink in that moment. Like someone letting the air escape from a balloon. He turned to Cadan.

'Do you have any idea who it may be, this traitor of yours?'

'No,' said Cadan. 'Not yet, but I will find them, I always do.'

Mawgan looked at Morwenna. She had gone very quiet. She was sitting on the edge of the massive bed with her eyes closed.

'This has happened before,' said Cadan. 'Many years ago, during the Pixie-Fae wars, a guardian sided with the Pixies and turned informant. They were dealt with.'

'How?'

Morwenna had a yellowish tinge to her face. She was starting to feel sick.

'They were exiled, expelled,' said Cadan. 'Their magic was taken from them, so they only had the knowledge of it, not its power or any means of using it. They were left to wander alone, not human, not Fae, not anything. They belonged nowhere and to no one.'

Morwenna knew only too well that feeling of alone. She was almost sorry for this new traitor. Whoever they were when Cadan found them, there would be no happy ending.

Later, when Mawgan and Morwenna entered the sitting-room again, they found Darcy, Kea and Glewas already asleep.

'At least they will get one more good night,' said Morwenna. 'I don't think I will ever sleep again.'

'I agree,' Mawgan nodded. 'But we must try at least. Tomorrow will be a very long day.'

The dawn arrived faster than any of them were prepared for; they were woken early and sat rubbing eyes and yawning before being ushered back into the dining room of the previous night for breakfast. Cadan walked in, followed by four more Fae.

'Are we done?' he asked.

He looked around the table. Mawgan nodded.

'Good, then let's go.'

They followed Cadan and the other Fae guards out of the palace. This time Darcy noticed her legs were very much under her own control. She didn't feel reassured by this as she walked behind Morwenna. As if sensing it, Morwenna dropped back and fell into step beside her.

'It's Ok Darcy, it really is. We can trust Cadan, he will help us.'

'You know him very well,' said Darcy.

'Why didn't you tell us you and Cadan are a thing?'

'We're not a thing,' replied Morwenna. 'We've not had a chance to be a thing, to be honest. Yes, you guessed right. We do have feelings for each other, strong feelings. But nothing has been acted on, and the possibility of that ever changing is slim. Very slim.'

'Why do you say that?' asked Darcy.

'Two reasons,' Morwenna replied. 'Nix and Hicca.'

Morwenna and Darcy walked on in silence for a while. Darcy could hear Kea and Glewas chatting in front of them, and Morgan was leading the party beside Cadan, also in deep discussion. Darcy looked at Morwenna. Even though they had been travelling for days now, without so much as a hairbrush between them, Morwenna still seemed tidy and pretty, despite her unkempt hair and rumpled clothing. Darcy had worked out that Cadan loved Morwenna. Just the way he looked at her, it was obvious.

They passed out of the palace gates. Kea tiptoed through, keeping well out of the way of the tiny grotesques, just in case. They were back in the woodland of the day before. Nothing seemed unusual or out of place, and they carried on, heading east for the best part of the morning. Darcy had discretely checked the compass last night while she, Kea and Glewas had been alone. It still read the same, directing her eastward through the Fae lands. She wondered to herself how she would explain a change of direction to Cadan if she ever needed to. She had been thinking about it over breakfast before she decided that was not just her concern, and Mawgan had probably already thought of an explanation if needed.

The morning passed, and they stopped for a quick bite to eat before carrying on. As they packed away what was left of the food. Glewas was startled by a sudden movement to his left.

'What was that?' he whispered to Kea beside him.

Kea was already reaching for the small knife he kept in his left boot. He slowly drew it out. The short blade bristled with his energy.

'Nothing,' said Glewas after a few seconds.

They carried on clearing until all traces of their lunch had gone. Cadan shuffled his boots through the dirt to mask their footprints. A flash of blue followed by a high-pitched giggle came from just to the right of him.

'They've found us,' said Mawgan.

Darcy was stunned at the speed of what happened next. The four Fae guards that had all morning, silently bringing up the rear of the company, sprung forward and surrounded Darcy and Morwenna. They threw up a magical force-field around them. Darcy and Morwenna were safe inside, but it also trapped them. They were helpless, unable to do anything other than watch what was happening around them. There were hundreds of Imps. They were fast, their movements erratic in a frenzy. Swarming in on the group from all sides, before Cadan, Mawgan, Kea and Glewas had any time to come up with any kind of strategy. They were smothered in the cloud of inky blue bodies and razor-sharp white teeth.

Darcy was screaming; she could hear the rasping, scraping sounds coming from her throat, but the noise seemed a separate thing from herself. That she was somewhere else, listening and watching.

Morwenna was casting protection charms beside Darcy but was becoming increasingly frustrated as they kept rebounding off whatever magic was in the force-field.

'Help them,' she screamed at the four guards.

They didn't move, they just kept on casting the field. Darcy realised whatever magic this was, it not only made them unreachable but also invisible and inaudible. The imps made no attempt to approach them. They had no idea they were there.

Darcy threw up. It was that stomach-churning, heart-wrenching type of vomiting that accompanies shock, abhorrence and helplessness. She had seen the imps before, the night Morwenna had been attacked. But this was much worse, worse than anything she could possibly imagine. She could hear moaning. She thought it was Kea making the sound, but there was no way of knowing for sure who it was underneath the blue mass.

A sudden explosion of light evaporated half the blue imps in one blast. It was Cadan, arms held high. Light was streaming outwards from his fingers. As the light touched one imp and then another, they melted away to nothing. Clear of the imps himself, he had rid Mawgan and Glewas of them. A weaselly, crusty voice called to them.

'Where's thi girl? We ken yi have her, all we want iz thi girl.'

Cadan's face was a violent red colour, his eyes burning.

'You have no business being here on Fae lands. Get back to the hell hole you crawled out from, all of you.'

Kea was moaning again; Darcy could see him now as the imps had moved off his face. He didn't look good at all. She called out to him, but he couldn't hear her from the other side of the force-field.

'What should we do?'

Darcy yelled at Morwenna beside her. Morwenna's hand was stretched out in front of her, fingertips touching the edge of the forcefield.

'Don't do that,' said the guard nearest to her.

'But we must help them,' said Morwenna. 'CADAN!'

Tears threw themselves down her face. There was so much moisture that her words gurgled.

'They are beyond your help, Morwenna Tredinnick,' said the guard. 'You must look after the girl, finish what has been started, help the girl.'

Morwenna looked at Darcy. She was so small, so young. But he was right, this was all about Darcy, everything had been for Darcy, and she must see it through to the end if she could.

Cadan, Glewas and Mawgan were busy dealing with the imp invasion as best they could. Kea, now unconscious, lay on the ground, imps scrabbling to and fro across his battered body.

No one saw Morwenna take Darcy by the hand and without so much as a word, lead her away deep into the woodland. The four guards held the force-field around them until they were well out of sight. When they could hold it no longer, they joined in the fighting. There was nothing more to be done.

'Where's thi girl?' said the same crusty voice. 'Yi widny leave her behind, yi ken where she iz. Give her ti me.'

The imp stood between them. He was taller than average for an imp, with a gnarled face and razor-sharp teeth unevenly arranged in his mouth. The teeth were made worse by the grimace that permanently contorted his face.

'She's with thi witch, isn't she?' he said.

The look on Glewas' face made the imp smile.

'I waz right, she iz with thi witch. Where are they?'

This time Glewas' face gave nothing away, distracted by his conversation, the imp had not seen Mawgan step up behind him, and with a wave of his hand he brought down on the Imps head a stream of sizzling electrical force. It instantly burnt him to a crisp right where he stood. All that was left were two smouldering footprints in the dirt. Cadan motioned with his hand, and a little wind took the ash of the imp and blew it away in a cloud of black. The other imps, realising that they were beaten, ran off into the wood.

Glewas, Cadan and Mawgan moved to where Kea was lying. He was motionless on the ground. His breath was coming quick and shallow in little bubbling gasps. Glewas knelt by Kea and lifted his head gently into his lap, holding it between his hands. Kea slowly opened his eyes and looked up. He tried to smile.

'Ee' got 'er away?' he said.

'Yes,' replied Glewas. 'Morwenna got her away from them.'

Kea grimaced.

'Try not to move,' Glewas said. 'We'll have you out of here in a jiffy.'

Kea looked up at him.

'I think ee' both know tha' isn't goin' to 'appen. Glewas.'

Kea grabbed at Glewas's hand.

''Ee 'ave to stop 'em gettin' back to Narcasta, and tellin' 'im where she is. 'Ee 'ave to stop the imps. If 'ee finds 'er then it's all been fer nothin', and it can't 'ave all be fer nothin'.'

Kea was finding it more and more difficult to breathe.

'Don't talk,' said Glewas, 'just rest. We will get the imps, nothing that has been done here has been for nothing'

A weak smile made its way slowly across Kea's face. He closed his eyes now. Thick blood was oozing from many points all over his body. He was so pale. Glewas thought he looked unusually fragile, that if he dropped him, he could break. Kea took one last struggling breath. It seemed to stop, suspended somehow in the air. Then his body gave in. He died in Glewas' arms.

Time stopped there in the woods. Glewas rocked his friend gently, holding him close. As if by doing so, he could keep Kea there. The only sound was a light breeze gently blowing through the treetops, Glewas shoulders moved up and down, beating time to his grief.

Mawgan placed a gentle hand on his shoulder.

'We must go Glewas. Cadan's guards will take care of Kea now and see to it he is returned home to his family. We must go on. It is what Kea wanted; it is what we must do.'

Glewas gently lay Kea's head back on the ground and got to his feet. Wiping his face on the back of his hand, he watched as Cadan's four guards now lifted Kea to their shoulders to bare him away back to the palace and prepare him for his last journey home. Glewas, Mawgan and Cadan watched on silently as the guards moved away towards the palace until they were out of sight.

Glewas turned to Mawgan.

'So, what now?' he asked.

'Now we go hunting imps,' replied Cadan.

Mawgan nodded.

'Yes, we must get them before they can relay any news of Darcy. It will be difficult, but I believe that between us we can manage it.'

'When do we meet up with Darcy and Morwenna?' Glewas asked.

'We don't,' replied Mawgan. 'It is better that they go on alone. Narcasta is looking for a large party, he will be less suspicious of two women alone, and we must do everything we can to ensure Darcy's success.'

Cadan looked suspiciously at Mawgan.

'I deduced that there must be more to this journey than you have let me know,' he said. 'Surely if I am to risk so much along with you both, it is only right that I should know the reason for that risk?'

Mawgan looked at Glewas, then he shook his head.

'No Cadan, it is better that as few as possible know our task, and I ask you old friend, to trust to our friendship of years past, I hope that this knowledge will be enough for you to want to help us.'

This time it was Cadan who looked on at the other two men.

'In years past, the wizards and the Fae have protected the peoples of Dumnonia. Even though they did not know that their very safety was often bought with the sacrifice of our blood. I have called you friend. No, more than that. I have called you brother, and I stand with you now. I will follow you and help in whatever way I can, and trusting to this brotherhood, I know that when the time is right, you will tell me why.'

Glewas nodded. He was too young to remember the bonds that had once existed between the Fae and the wizards, but he had heard the stories. A dim recollection was stirring in the recesses of his mind now. It was too far out of his grasp yet, a memory of a story he had been told as a child but couldn't quite recall. He only knew that it was relevant and that he had an odd feeling about it. The feeling niggled at him, but he didn't yet understand why.

Weaving on through the tangled mass of tree roots and ancient oaks that seemed to make their path unbearably slow going and hard to navigate, Cadan led Glewas and Mawgan hour by hour. They walked for the most part in silence. They were acutely aware of every broken twig, every sound, no matter how small, a possible sign they may be on the right trail. That they may find imps at any moment and what that could mean for them. The three had one significant advantage, one that Kea had not shared. Magic. Mawgan and Glewas possessed it, and Cadan was the very embodiment of it. Magic made them sensitive to many aspects of the natural world that remained hidden to those without it. Mawgan was at that moment using his magical third eye. It wasn't an actual eye, more like another sixth sense. It was a combination of all the senses. He could see, smell, touch, hear and taste the world around him in such detail that it enabled him to see the ripples any moving object makes as it moves through space.

He was looking directly at a ripple now. It was barely there, but it was there, and he knew it had been made by many fast, small things as they ran through the woods. Cadan and Glewas saw it too, and the knowledge of what it meant passed unsaid between the three of them. Picking up their pace, they followed the ripple. Slowly and steadily, it became more pronounced. They were gaining on them.

Within half an hour of first noticing the ripple in space, Cadan, Mawgan and Glewas had their first sight of the imps. They were fast as lightning, but that wasn't fast enough. Cadan raised his hand and took care of three back runners in an electrifying shockwave. Realising now that they were under attack, the imps formed a circle around the two wizards and Cadan. This did not have the desired effect of surrounding and cutting off the enemy from any escape route. What it did was make things a whole lot easier for Cadan to eliminate them imp by imp as he swung around in an arc, light pouring from his outstretched hand. Each imp exploded in turn as soon as the light touched their skin. On seeing what was happening to the other imps, a particularly nasty creature on the edge of the pack snuck backwards and out of the circle. Picking up his pace, he ran, unnoticed by Cadan, Mawgan and Glewas. The imp had to get to his master and had no feeling of obligation to help the others. The message had to get through. That was the only important thing.

'That was easy,' said Glewas when it was over.

'A bit too easy,' said Mawgan.

Cadan nodded in agreement.

'Yes, there must be a reason, it was as if they were distracting us from something.'

Glewas looked carefully about him. There were many small footprints all around the area, it was difficult to make any sense of them, only they had the advantage that they already knew what had taken place there. As Glewas looked further, he noticed another set of footprints. These were not like the others, they were facing in another direction altogether, away from the fighting.

'Look at this! These prints are running away,' said Glewas.

Mawgan and Cadan looked for themselves. Sure enough, Glewas was right.

'Damn it!' said Mawgan. 'We missed one.'

'One is all it will take,' said Glewas. 'We've failed them. Kea, Darcy and Morwenna, we've failed them all.'

He looked at the ground, clutching his chest. Defeated. Glewas thought his heart would burst with the pain of it all. Kea first, and now Darcy. A girl he had only just met. Now she was the most important person in the world to him, and he hadn't even had the chance to tell her.

'Come on,'

Cadan slapped Glewas on the back.

'This isn't going to fix anything, we can either stay here and feel sorry about everything that's happened, or we can track this stray and get to him before Narcasta does. What's it going to be?'

Mawgan looked at Glewas, his head on one side.

'Well?' he said.

Glewas sniffed, cleared his throat and looked at the two men. They too had experienced losses. They were in this together, and there was some amount of comfort in that.

'Let's get this bugger,' he said.

Glewas had made his choice. They all had. There was no going back now for any of them. With a smile and a nod, Cadan turned to follow the Imp trail, closely followed by Glewas and Mawgan. Today they had an imp to catch.

CHAPTER ELEVEN

DONYARTH

Morwenna had to pull Darcy along beside her as they ran.

'Stop!' Darcy pleaded. 'We have to go back, we have to help them.'

Morwenna came to a sharp stop.

'There is nothing we can do,' she said. 'We have to make their sacrifice mean something. If we go back, then you will be taken, and there will have been no point to all of this. If they are sacrificing themselves to save you at this very moment, then that sacrifice must make a difference.'

Morwenna's eyes. Darcy had never seen anyone look like that. She didn't know how to begin to describe it. All her arguments, her reasoning on why they shouldn't be running away just left her. She had nothing more to say.

'Come on,' said Morwenna, 'we need to keep moving.'

She grabbed Darcy's hand again, but this time, Darcy didn't struggle.

They moved quickly and in silence. After an hour, Morwenna stopped.

'Check the compass.'

Morwenna bent over, hands on her knees for support. She threw up. Darcy pulled on the chain around her neck until the compass popped out of her coat. It was now reading south east. She turned to Morwenna.

'It's changed, and I have just realised something.'

'What's that?' Morwenna replied, straitening up.

'It's just that if we head southeast, as the compass is telling us to now, that will take us right back to where we started. We will have travelled full circle. Do you think that when Mawgan sealed the gateway at Tintagel, when I got stuck here, that something happened, that the gateway didn't close properly?'

Morwenna still felt sick. But all she was doing was dry retching. There wasn't anything left to come up. She straightened and took a few deep breaths, wiping her mouth with her hand.

'I don't know, there are so many things that could have happened or gone wrong. Eclipses are strange and have powers none of us really understand. Maybe it didn't close. I guess we'll all know soon enough. Ready?'

Darcy nodded.

'Yes, I think I have my breath back.'

'Right then,' said Morwenna, 'let's go.'

They turned and ran south east.

Cadan, Glewas and Mawgan followed the trail of the imp deeper into the wood. It would fade now and then, but for the most part, it wasn't difficult to track. Mawgan expressed his concern that the imp was heading straight to Tintagel and Narcasta, Cadan agreed. They upped their effort to reach it before it had the chance to complete its task.

An hour later they had the imp in their sights. It was running quick, but it wasn't fast enough to escape them. Cadan drew level with it on one side, with Glewas coming up on the other. They waited as Mawgan came in from the rear and the three of them pulled in closer and closer. They almost had the imp in their reach when there was a small implosion. A tiny black speck in space opened just ahead of it. The imp lunged, vanishing instantly. The speck right along with it. They were gone.

'What just happened?' Glewas yelled.

'The damn thing teleported,' said Cadan. 'We must be nearer Narcasta than I had realised. Teleportation can only be done within a few miles of the intended destination. That's it. We're too late. He knows everything.'

They moved on through the wood a little further. Sure enough, the trees became fewer and less dense until the three found themselves on the open moor.

'Donyarth,' said Mawgan.

An involuntary shiver ran right down Glewas' back.

'I hate this place,' he said.

Darcy was exhausted. She felt that her lungs were about to explode. They burned in her chest with the effort of getting enough oxygen into her body. Any moment she was going to be sick or faint or something.

'I have to stop,' she said.

Morwenna slowed.

'Yes, let's rest for a while.'

They plonked themselves on the ground. Darcy took out the compass again. Yes, it was still reading south east. They were heading straight back to Tintagel. Darcy frowned. Something very bad was about to happen. She had realised over her time in Dumnonia that she had a good sense for these things. This was her sixth sense. She didn't have the magic as the others did, but she had the feelings, strong feelings. And she was learning to trust in them. Maybe that was why she was the bearer of the compass. This sixth sense that she was discovering may be the reason that she was here instead of another.

Morwenna got up and looked around.

'I know this place.'

She was reassuring herself as much as Darcy.

She moved off again, and Darcy struggled to her feet, not quite getting up quick enough.

'Wait for me,' Darcy called.

But Morwenna was gone.

Darcy took hold of the compass, still on its chain around her neck. She clutched at it tightly.

'If ever I needed the power to feel what's going to happen next, it's now.'

She gathered all her strength and moved on, keeping a careful watch for Morwenna or anything else that could be hiding in the gloominess under the trees.

The surrounding trees began to thin out until they were so sparse. The fear of discovery was making her breath catch in her throat. As she broke out of the cover of the trees. The daylight was almost gone. She had not realised how dark it had become until now. Out from the trees she could see the moon, clearly risen well above the horizon, it's watery light illuminated the ground around her.

'Oh, no. Bodmin Moor.'

Darcy shivered.

'Well?'

Narcasta warmed himself in front of a weak fire. The heat and smoke from it combined in a sickly thick cloud above his head. He coughed.

'A have seen them master,' said the imp.

He bent over, holding his knees, which were still wobbling ridiculously. The little blue body was unable to recover from its sudden jump via the teleportation hole moments before.

'A have led them ta thi place,' he said.

'And the girl is with them?' said Narcasta.

'There were only two wizards, a Faerie and a boy,' said the imp. 'Thi otha boy iz ni more. It was vere satisfying ta take him.'

The imp grinned and licked his dry lips. Narcasta put his hand over his mouth and closed his eyes. He moved closer to the fire.

'We didny see thi girl,' said the imp.

'She must be there,' said Narcasta.

His eyes were still closed. He rubbed the temples of his forehead with two index fingers so bony and white; it was impossible to tell if they had any skin coverage at all.

'Mawgan would not have left her behind. She is too important, too valuable. They hid her from you. You fool.'

His white hand swiped across the top of the imp's bald blue head.

'A–er–A was just about ta say. Thi witch, she was gone too. Thi young wizard couldny hide it, they are together, a'd stake mi life on it.'

The stammering imp dared not look up.

'Good,' said Narcasta. 'I might just need to take you up on that.'

The imp's Adam's Apple bobbed up and down as he swallowed hard. He took a step back, then vanished again with a little pop.

'So, you have come to me as I planned.'

Narcasta stopped tracing the circular pattern above his eyes. The headache was dissipating. There was another popping sound, and he too was gone.

The hill was dark. Silhouetted against the sky were stones, many stones. Cold, they had a brooding presence, a physical force. If you reached out, you would touch that force, whatever it was, and it would mean death. Darcy shivered. It was an involuntary response to a feeling that she had been in this place before, that she had lived this moment in the past somehow, déjà vu. For some reason, she had the most definite feeling that Mawgan would be here. Darcy looked about frantically.

'Where could he be?'

There were few places to hide and the stones; no one in their right mind would get near any of them. Darcy felt that at any moment they would move and grab for her and she would be gone. She didn't know where, but she had no intention of finding out. Like a light clicking on in her brain, she suddenly remembered the dream. The second night at the caravan park, Darcy had dreamt of this place, this moment. That's why she had thought that she had been here before, and that's how Darcy knew Mawgan would be here too. She had already seen him here.

Morwenna touched her arm.

'There you are,' she said. 'I thought I had lost you for good.'

'Morwenna!'

Darcy turned to meet her.

'I've seen this place before,'

'I'm not surprised,' said Morwenna. 'I understand it also exists in your world; I've always found it to be a strange place. It only seems to be at peace at midsummer, the rest of the year it has a presence I don't like.'

'No, that's not it,' said Darcy. 'I've seen this in a dream I had when I first came to Cornwall. Mawgan's here somewhere, too. We have to find him.'

Morwenna and Darcy searched for Mawgan amongst the stones.

'If Mawgan is here,' said Morwenna, 'then surely the others must be here too?'

'I don't know,' Darcy replied, 'in my dream, I only saw Mawgan.'

A chilling realisation spread through Darcy's mind. If she had only seen Mawgan in her dream, did that mean something terrible had happened to Cadan, Kea and Glewas? Morwenna must have been having the same thoughts because she called out, frantically hoping that someone would answer. They did.

'For goodness' sake, be quiet will you,' Glewas hissed. 'You're enough to wake the dead with all that racket.'

He pulled Morwenna and Darcy down to hide beside him, behind the remains of an old fallen tree.

'Why do we need to be quiet?' asked Darcy.

Glewas looked from Morwenna to Darcy and back again.

'Because He's coming.'

'He who?' asked Morwenna.

Darcy saw the look on Glewas' face.

'He, Narcasta?' said Darcy. 'Where are the others?'

'Cadan and Mawgan are just over there,' said Glewas.

Pointing to his left.

'And Kea? Where's Kea?'

Morwenna was looking directly at Glewas' face as she asked her question, and immediately, she saw the answer in his eyes.

'No!'

The word was almost a sob as it left her mouth.

'Glewas, where's Kea?' said Darcy.

'He's gone, Darcy,'

The speaking of those words brought such emotion to Glewas's face. Tears streamed down his cheeks. He took Darcy's hand and continued.

'We lost him in the imp attack, back in the woods. He tried to hold on, he was strong, but it wasn't enough. I couldn't save him.'

'Don't blame yourself for this,' Morwenna said. 'There is someone to blame, but it isn't you. There was nothing any of us could have done. We saw the attack too. It was brutal and fast and over before any of us really knew what was happening.'

'We left him.'

This was all that Darcy said.

'Yes, we did,' Morwenna replied. 'Because if we hadn't, then it might very well have been YOU lying there covered in imps, and right now it would all be over. Narcasta would have you and the compass, and that would be the end of it.'

They didn't speak any more. There was nothing more to say. Darcy cried quietly by Glewas' side as she and Morwenna huddled down with him behind the old fallen tree. A movement to their left made Morwenna start. It was Mawgan and Cadan. On seeing him, Morwenna fell into Cadan's arms.

'I thought you might be dead,' she cried.

'No, my lovely, I'm still very much alive.'

He bent and kissed her forehead. As he did so, she noticed the scratches on his face and suddenly had a rush of feeling. He had put himself on the line, for her, for Darcy, for all of them. He had shown up when it mattered most, and she loved him for it.

From behind one of the stones, Narcasta made himself visible. He was huge, at least as tall as Cadan, but there was one immediately noticeable difference. Instead of the beautiful Fae face, there was a scarred, gnarled skull, but it was alive. It was barely covered by skin, its eyes sunken, lips shrivelled. His long hair greasy and scraped back against the top of the head. If he was trying to look scary, then he was successful.

Even though her fear was by this point almost overwhelming, Darcy was still looking at Narcasta while she remained out of sight behind the tree. Why had she compared him with Cadan? Why was that the obvious comparison? As if reading her thoughts, Mawgan was between Glewas and herself. He had arrived by the tree just after Cadan and put his arm around her, protectively.

'So now you have seen him for what he is then,' he said, 'this evil of our own making.'

'What do you mean?' asked Darcy.

'Banished from his people, his family. His magic transformed into some lesser thing, his hate consumed him, he became this being that you see now. Once Narcasta was fair, handsome, a creature created by magic, he was magic itself. Jealous of the elder brother he both loved and hated, he made a deal with the enemy that if he helped them, and they were successful, he would take his brother's place and rule. But the plan was discovered before it could be carried out. So here he is, the banished younger brother of our very own Fae lord, now a burden all of Dumnonia must carry.'

Darcy stared at Mawgan.

'You mean to tell me that this Narcasta is Cadan's brother; that he's Fae?'

'Yes and no,' Mawgan replied. 'He is Cadan's brother. There is no denying that, but he is Fae no longer. That was taken from him, along with everything that Narcasta had once been or ever could be. This is all that is left now, this is what it looks like to be nothing, a mere spark of what you once were. When everything good and fine is removed, this is what's left.'

'I know you are here, gatekeeper,' Narcasta's voice resonated around the stones.

Darcy felt she was freezing, her body shivering and her fingers and toes, numb. She remembered this. This was the coldness she had felt the day her family had driven through Bodmin moor. She had experienced the cold again the night she had dreamed about this place. Darcy grabbed hold of Mawgan's hand.

'Darcy!' said Mawgan, 'you're freezing.'

'It's his voice,' Darcy explained. 'For some reason, I have a physical reaction to it. My blood literally runs cold.'

Glewas wrapped his arms around her, and Mawgan's face pinched with concern.

'What is it?' Glewas said, looking at Mawgan's expression.

'I'm not sure,' said Mawgan.

He wrapped his hand over the top of Darcy's.

'It seems she has some sought of physical connection with Narcasta. Why had I not seen this?'

Mawgan muttered to himself something inaudible, then looking at Glewas.

'When we consulted the head of our order, there was no mention that this could happen.'

Glewas thought for a moment.

'They may not have known. Don't forget, Darcy is not from this world, maybe this is not just her reaction to him, maybe this is how everyone in that world will react, frozen. He must not get through.'

Mawgan thought a bit more.

'Magic is not the same in that world; it is more subtle, less of a spectacle and based heavily in the knowledge of things. Here Darcy's reaction is physical. There, well, it may be more emotional. If she is frozen here, maybe there, her reaction would be indifference or apathy. This is very dangerous, indeed. You are right, Glewas, he must never get through.'

'I want the girl Gatekeeper. Give her to me, and I will be lenient with the rest of you.'

Narcasta's voice rang out. Darcy's teeth were chattering with cold, and her lips had gone a funny shade of blue-tinged purple.

'This can't go on Mawgan,' said Glewas. 'He's killing her.'

Mawgan placed his hands on Darcy's head, closed his eyes and breathing deeply, he whispered,

'Baernan.'

Darcy felt the change immediately in her fingers and toes. A tingle, followed by a slow thawing. The sensation moved up her arms and legs into the rest of her body, inch by warming inch until apart from flushed cheeks, she was her usual colour again. Mawgan removed his hands.

'There, that should do it.'

'Wow,' said Darcy, rubbing her hands together. 'How did you do that?'

Mawgan looked incredulous.

'Magic can be used in many ways, Darcy. Don't look so surprised that it was able to help you.'

'I'm not surprised,' Darcy replied. 'I knew you could fix me, I just wanted to know how.'

'If you have all finished, perhaps we could deal with the task at hand.' said Cadan. 'This is my problem, I must be the one to deal with Narcasta, you must get Darcy away and home.'

Mawgan raised his eyebrows.

'Yes, Mawgan, I have guessed that she has a compass. How else would you have expected to get her home?

For far too long a time, I have allowed others to deal with a problem I created, now I must deal with Narcasta once and for all. You must complete your task, get Darcy away, and close the gate. I take it you still have some of the catalyst left?'

'Yes,' Mawgan replied. 'Darcy still has it in her bag.'

'Then go now,' said Cadan. 'I will cause a distraction, and you will be able to escape. Take the young wizard with you, Morwenna will stay with me. She and I will not be separated again.'

Morwenna nodded her head in agreement, and Mawgan saw she had made up her mind to stay with Cadan, whatever that meant.

Cadan rose to his feet from behind the old fallen tree and moved out to the centre of a stone circle. The moon shone off his glossy black hair, his extremely tall frame cast a long shadow on the ground behind him.

'Ah, brother,' said Narcasta as he too moved into the centre of the circle.

There they both were, the light and the dark, yet the similarities were also undeniable. These were Darcy's thoughts as she, Glewas and Mawgan crept on all fours to the other end of the long, rotting trunk they were hiding behind.

'When I give the word,' Mawgan whispered, 'get ready to run for it.'

Darcy stole a look back at Cadan and Narcasta deep in conversation, then turned to Mawgan and nodded.

'Ok,' Glewas whispered from behind 'we'll be ready.'

He once again took Darcy's hand.

'We'll need to move quickly, hold on to me and don't let go.'

At that moment, Darcy stole a look to the other end of the rotting trunk where Morwenna was still hiding. She was totally engrossed in what was playing out between Cadan and Narcasta. She didn't see the movement just behind her as Barrowman crept up towards her.

Everything that happened next happened so quickly it's almost a blur in Darcy's memory.

'Look out!' she cried.

The moment the words left her mouth, Darcy knew it was a mistake. Barrowman turned to face her now.

'Got you,' he growled.

Narcasta also heard Darcy and dodged away from Cadan, lunging towards the sound of her voice. Glewas grabbed at Darcy's hand and pulled her with him away from the tree and off behind Mawgan into the dark. There was no time to think, only an irrepressible instinct to run was all that filled Darcy's mind. Barrowman was right with them now. Darcy could smell the stale tang of his sweat and hear his laboured breathing. He sounded like a colossal dog in the dark behind her. Darcy ran fast, but he kept pace, and they couldn't shake him off. Mawgan, determined for them to get away, grabbed Darcy's other hand to help Glewas move her along faster, but it was no use, Barrowman increased his pace and grabbed at Darcy's coat from behind. The first grab missed by millimetres, his second grab found the coat's hood, and he yanked Darcy backwards towards him. Darcy felt her hands slip from Mawgan and Glewas' grasp, and the next things she felt were the arms of Barrowman as he held her and ran off in a different direction into the night. There was a popping sound just ahead of them, Darcy saw in that split second that Narcasta was there, he had made what looked like a small hole in space. It was darker than the night around it, and he and Barrowman still holding Darcy ran into the hole and were gone. The hole collapsed behind them, and there was nothing but still night once more.

The sound that Glewas made on seeing Darcy disappear was like the sound a wounded animal might make; it wasn't so much a cry, more a howl. Mawgan was right with him. He placed a hand on Glewas' shoulder in some effort to comfort him, but his own distress at what had happened was equally powerful. A few seconds later, Cadan and Morwenna came upon them. Immediately understanding the situation, Cadan voiced what everyone else was thinking.

'Well, that's it,' he said, 'it's over. Narcasta has Darcy. More than that, he has a compass. There will be no stopping him now.'

'How could I have been so stupid?'

Mawgan chastised himself aloud.

'He was just the distraction to keep us from seeing Barrowman. By the time Darcy had seen him, it was too late.'

'Do not be so hard on yourself,' Cadan told him. 'I too didn't see his deception, I thought I would be his distraction and allow you to get Darcy away; instead, he was mine. His deviousness increases, I underestimated him.'

Darcy stood in a dark room. The only light came from a fire that smouldered feebly in its blackened grate. She looked around. The walls were rough-hewn stone. She noticed that soot clung to them in damp, oozing patches. There was the smell of mould in the air, it was an ancient foulness. Darcy held her breath for a moment; she worried she would catch something from breathing in the atmosphere of the room. Darcy realised how ridiculous that was, she couldn't stop breathing; what was the alternative? She shivered and pulled the thin blanket she had been given tighter around her; it didn't help. They had stripped her of most of her clothes so there could be no place to hide anything, but Darcy hadn't anything left to hide. When Barrowman had snatched her, she had struggled and squirmed so much, that before they had disappeared into the black hole, she had been able to do two things without him noticing. She had pulled the compass from around her neck and stuffed it into the rucksack containing Jenna's bag; then she had dropped the bag in the darkness without him seeing or hearing it fall. Her only chance now was that one of the others had found it.

The witch's tattooed hand was on the door as she pushed her way slowly into the room where Darcy was being held. She was a crone in appearance, and Darcy recalled all the fairy stories she had been told that featured a witch; the old woman was exactly what she had pictured.

'My name is Tryfena,' the woman said.

Her voice crackled. Darcy pushed herself back against one of the walls, trying to put as much space as possible between herself and the old woman.

'Where is it?' the woman continued. 'What have you done with the compass?'

'I don't know what you're talking about,' said Darcy.

'Oh, I think you know, child,' Tryfena said. 'Mawgan was searching for a way to get you back home. The only means to accomplish such a thing, is by finding a gateway with a compass. You had a compass, that's why your little group has been wandering about the countryside. You have been searching for a gateway, and here you are.'

Tryfena smiled. It was a toothless grin that did nothing to brighten her face or make her look any less disturbing.

'Now, why is it you are back here again?'

The question was as much directed at herself as at Darcy. Tryfena thought for a moment.

'Could it be that Mawgan failed? Yes, that's it. Mawgan failed. The gate is still open.'

Tryfena didn't need Darcy to answer. She turned, remarkably quickly for such an old woman and left the room, slamming the door behind her as she went. Darcy heard a lock turn, and she was alone once again.

Darcy tried to sleep, but her eyes would not stay closed. As she sat in the darkness of her cell, she knew only two things. She was freezing, and she was very alone.

CHAPTER TWELVE

BIRTHDAYS

There are two types of birthdays. Those that are so uneventful they never stir you to remember one second of the day, totally melded into the recesses of your mind, marked 'unnecessary' and 'ok to forget'. Then, there are those where every moment is indelibly inked into your brain, a slow-motion movie reel ready to be played repeatedly in the picture house of your mind. Darcy found the latter true of her fourteenth birthday, though how she even got to celebrate it, remains a total mystery to her.

'Can 'ee see anythin' Hicca?'

Nix called to him as she hid behind the crenulations of the castle's rooftop. Hicca was peering over the top, trying to make out where the posted guards were currently situated. He was determined not to run into any of them if they could be possibly avoided. Narcasta's henchmen were nasty, particularly Barrowman. There was no way Hicca wanted to run into him.

'There's no one abou',' said Hicca, 'I can' see anythin'.'

'Where 'ee heck are they?' said Nix. 'This place is usually crawlin' in scum.'

'They mus' be busy,' said Hicca, 'which is good fer us. Let's go.'

Just a few hours before, both the pixies had been on the moor. They had arrived in time to see Barrowman grab Darcy and disappear with her. They had also seen Darcy drop the bag she was carrying.

Nix had picked it up and now had it safely swung over her shoulder. Finding the rest of the party together, they had quickly come up with what could, very loosely, be called 'a plan', and now they were here on the castle roof attempting to carry it out or die trying.

Seeing Narcasta use a black hole to teleport Darcy, Barrowman and himself into the castle, had given Cadan the idea that if they could get in that way, it made perfect sense that they could also use the same method to get Darcy out. It took all of Hicca's self-control to accept that the faerie had a good plan, but Nix had long suspected Morwenna's secret liking for him and persuaded Hicca that it was the right thing to do and the plan was sound. While Nix and Hicca snuck into the castle to find Darcy, the others made their way to the walled gardens and the gateway. The plan was that eventually, they would all meet up there. Darcy would, at last, go home, and Mawgan would seal the gateway permanently.

'We have to find one of 'em,' said Hicca. 'I don't know where they'll be hiding her, so you need to have a good listen in on them and see if you can't work it out.'

Nix nodded in agreement. They both transformed into light and floated down into the belly of the castle just in time to see Tryfena rushing along a dark corridor, looking like she had some important news to tell. They followed her down the hallway, up a flight of stone steps and into and into a smokey chamber where Narcasta was waiting for her.

'Well?' he asked. 'What have you discovered?'

'Oh master,' Tryfena said, 'it is better than we had hoped. The girl did have a compass, although she does not have it now. The compass led them back here. Which can only mean one thing. The Gatekeeper was not able to seal the gateway, it is still open. All that remains for us to do is to discover which one of them now has the compass and take it; then you can go straight through.'

Narcasta rested his chin heavily on his hands as he thought for a moment. A satisfied smile spread slowly across his face.

'Thank you, Tryfena,' he said, 'you have been most helpful, but you can go now, I won't need your services again.'

'Yes master,' Tryfena replied, as she left the room with a low bow.

The smile on Narcasta's face continued to grow.

'So brother, you finally have possession of what you have always wanted. I know it is you who has the compass. The girl looked to keep it from me, but in doing so has delivered it to you. The question is, will you be able to resist its power? We shall see.'

Narcasta rose to his feet and leaving the room bellowed.

'Barrowman, come, we're leaving.'

'Idiot!' Nix muttered under her breath when Narcasta had left.

'As if 'ee would give the compass to a faerie, no matter how good 'ee may be. Well, Narcasta will find a nice reception committee waitin' fer 'im in the garden.'

'Come on, Nix,' Hicca interrupted, ''ee needs to find Darcy.'

Nix thought for a moment.

'When 'ee first saw Tryfena, she was in that corridor downstairs, that's where Darcy'll be, I'd bet anythin' on it.'

They both floated back to the corridor and looked in every room until they came to a securely locked door.

'That'll be the one,' said Nix.

She floated into the lock space. There was a little click, and the door swung inwards. Darcy blinked in the light from the doorway.

'Oh, you poor darlin',' Nix exclaimed.

She entered the room and transformed into her full size.

'let's see what we can do fer 'ee.'

Before long Nix had found some clothes for Darcy and some water so she could wash her face.

'Are 'ee ready to go yet?'

Hicca called from his position of guard at the doorway.

'Yes, yes' Nix cried, pushing Darcy towards the door.

'Are 'ee ready?' asked Hicca.

'Ready for what?' Darcy replied, worry on her face.

Hicca took one of her hands and Nix the other.

'This.'

They both said together as they swept her up in a wisp of magic light and were gone.

The garden was precisely the way Darcy remembered it the night she had come through the gateway. The rose bushes that had hidden her from Narcasta were much the same, and she hid behind them now. When she had arrived in the garden with Nix and Hicca, the others were already there. Morwenna had given her the biggest hug, her relief at Darcy's return very visible in her face. Glewas too. Mawgan had more practical matters on his mind.

'I need the catalyst if you please, Darcy,' he said, 'and if you're ready, it's time for you to go; say your goodbyes.'

Darcy rooted around in Jenna's bag, she handed Mawgan the bottle of potion, there wasn't much left, she hoped it would be enough.

Mawgan looked at it quizzically for a moment, then tucked it in his pocket. She felt for the compass, and once she had found it hung it around her neck once more. The pointer immediately stopped its spinning and aligned itself with a space on the far wall.

'There it is!' said Mawgan.

Sure enough, as he was saying the words, the gateway appeared in the darkness, its door slightly ajar.

'Now Darcy,' Mawgan coaxed her gently, 'its time.'

Darcy hugged Nix, Hicca and once again Morwenna; she turned to Glewas to do the same, but instead of a hug, he gently took her face in his hands and kissed her. At that moment they were alone, everything else in the garden just melted away.

'I'll never forget you.,' he whispered against her hair.

She felt the heat of his breath against her ear, and it tingled.

'Don't you dare forget me.'

'No,' she whispered back. She looked deep into his eyes. 'Never.'

Glewas let her go, stepped away and Cadan placed a hand on her head.

'Go, child,' he said, 'be happy, and remember us.'

Darcy nodded, and she and Mawgan moved towards the gateway.

There was a sudden commotion behind them. Darcy found herself being flung against a stone wall as Mawgan pushed her out of the way. Narcasta now had hold of Mawgan. His hands around his throat, he lifted him clear off the ground. Mawgan was choking, and Darcy was helpless. Narcasta was massive, far beyond her strength, but she rushed at his ankles and bit into one for all she was worth. He roared and dropped Mawgan, who fell like a stone, forming a crumpled heap on the ground. Cadan was suddenly there; he had come up from behind. And now had placed his right hand on the back of Narcasta's head. What looked like a surge of electricity buzzed between his fingers and Narcasta's body; the power surging through him made Narcasta glow. Darcy thought if it hadn't been so terrible, it would have looked beautiful. His whole body glowed with light.

Morwenna fought for all she was worth, Barrowman was big, but he was also clumsy, his size slowed him down enough to give the nimble witch the advantage. She cast every protective charm she had ever memorised, even the ones she struggled with and were not her best. Morwenna was battling for her life, but she was holding him off. It was working. Nix and Hicca had just finished dealing with Tryfena, she had been an easy fix, ancient and decrepit, the witch was no match for two pixies and had quickly been reduced to a smouldering pile of ashes on the ground. Finished with Tryfena, they now came up beside Morwenna and beat down Barrowman with a barrage of magical force that had him begging for them to stop. Nix and Hicca, realising the wizard henchman was surrendering, stopped. They held him where he was, immobile, helpless and obviously sulking.

Cadan sunk to his knees. He had no strength left. It had taken every ounce of him to take on his brother, not just physical but emotional too. Whatever Narcasta had done, whatever evil he still had planned, there was a connection of blood, of shared memories of better times. Narcasta's body still had a residual glow of the energy that until moments before had surged through it, he didn't move. Mawgan, who had recovered somewhat from being strangled, prodded at the body tentatively, trying to assess its level of risk to them all.

'Is 'ee dead?' asked Nix, coming alongside him.

'I don't think so,' said Mawgan.

He prodded at Narcasta again.

'Not 'im,' said Nix, ''ee other one.'

She was looking at Cadan, who had fallen over now and was lying on one side with his eyes closed and a very grey tone to his skin. Morwenna arrived by his side, she stroked his cheek with the back of her forefinger, Nix drew in a sharp breath through clenched teeth, it had the unfortunate effect of sounding very much like a hiss.

'It won't work mother.'

Morwenna said to her, all her attention still focussed on Cadan.

'It's too late, I love him. I don't want a fuss, there's nothing you or Hicca can do to change it, he's mine.'

She stroked Cadan's perspiration-soaked hair and finally looked at Nix, who saw at that moment, the fierce determination in her daughter's eyes.

Nix nodded her head at Morwenna, realising the futility of any counterargument. Cadan stirred, groaning with the effort. He got into a sitting position with Morwenna's help. Nix placed her hand over his forehead. Closing her eyes in concentration, she let magic leave her body and transfer to Cadan. As Morwenna looked on, Cadan's condition improved. He lost the pale grey tinge to his skin. His strength slowly returning. Nix finished her ministrations and removed her hand from Cadan's head.

'Thank you,' he said,

'I didn't do it fer 'ee,' said Nix.

Cadan nodded.

'I know,' he said, 'but thank you all the same.'

Slowly, he moved over to where Mawgan was sitting, still prodding Narcasta unceremoniously in the ribs.

'He's not dead, Mawgan,' Cadan said.

Mawgan withdrew his hand sharply back into his cloak.

'What did you do to him?' Mawgan asked.

'I pushed everything I had through him,' Cadan explained. 'All my power, it was all I could think of.'

'Well, it worked,' said Mawgan. 'You shorted him out.'

'I did what?' asked Cadan.

'It's a thing from Darcy's world,' continued Mawgan. 'It's too complicated to explain right now. What will you do with him?'

'I'll take him home,' Cadan replied. 'I don't know if anything can be done to change him, help him, but I will try. This is a Fae problem, and the Fae will deal with him. It should have always been that way, but I lost a sense of who I was in everything that happened. I stopped caring about how my decisions were affecting the lives of so many others. I didn't see it, I closed it off. Then I met Morwenna, everything changed, I realised how my decision affected them, affected her, affected people she loves. I couldn't allow it anymore. This is putting it right. I only hope she will forgive me.'

'She will,' said Mawgan. looked across at Morwenna.

'I think she already has.' Mawgan moved from his position and stood up. 'Darcy,' he said.

It was barely above a whisper, but she heard him.

'It's time.'

Darcy turned to Mawgan.

'Promise you'll visit me sometimes,' she said.

'I'm afraid this really is goodbye,' Mawgan replied, 'once the gateway is sealed, it cannot be reopened. That also means mind twinning will no longer be possible either. I will always remember our time, my lovely girl, and how you helped, what you risked, you are an extraordinary person to all of us, and most especially to me.'

Mawgan hugged her so fiercely she thought her bones might break. Then he held her away from him.

'Off you go now,' he said.

Darcy turned to the place she had last seen the gateway. Sure enough, it was still there. Mawgan made ready with the potion behind her.

He came out of nowhere; one moment, he had been immobilised with an angry Pixie sitting on his back, pinning him down with both weight and magic. The next moment he had thrown off his captor and in one smooth movement, which was very unlike him, had closed the distance between where he was held captured and where Darcy was now moving towards the gateway. Darcy spun around. She had no time to think; it was a totally reflexive move; she pushed her pointing finger into the socket of his right eye, as hard as she could. It gave a little pop, and Barrowman let out a roar. Seizing this small opportunity, Darcy flung herself at the gateway. This was her only chance. She could see Mawgan, Cadan and the Pixies as if everything was happening in slow motion. They were quickly catching up with the situation, but not quick enough to stop Barrowman. She could feel the pull now of the gateway, drawing her in and away. Barrowman's hand closed around a piece of her jacket collar. It slipped on the fabric, tearing as it went. As she fell back, she felt a sharp tug at her neck; it was excruciating. For a second, it felt like a white-hot cord was slicing through it, but only for a second. She heard a ping, so minuscule, it was barely audible, and then the pain was gone and so was the compass.

The first thing Darcy noticed was a thin line of brightness. It ran across the middle of her vision and grew wider. She wondered what it could be. Considering her options, she closed her eyes tight and opened them again to see if it helped. It didn't; the brightness was now unbearable. Blinking, her eyes closed, open, closed, open. Her vision eventually adjusted enough for the light to not be the blinding sensation it had first been. She could now make out shapes, a window, a door, she was in a room, a pristine, white room. She tried to move her head to take in more of her surroundings.

'*Ouch.*'

That really hurt. Darcy moved her arms, but her left felt like a dead weight. She looked down her body and noticed the white cast that encased the arm. It was then that she realised she was lying flat on a soft surface, a bed. Her head was fuzzy; her brain was taking longer to assess things than it would generally. She could hear muffled sounds beside her. She tried to focus; the sounds seemed familiar, but they also seemed far off or like hearing underwater.

'*Focus, Darcy,*' she said to herself.

The sounds started to clear; she did recognise them. They were voices; as familiar to her as her own.

'Darcy, can you hear me?' said Tom. 'Pippa, she's opening her eyes; call the nurse, quickly.'

A team of medical people rushed into the room and started to check pulses, observe reactions to stimulation and check monitors. Pippa held the hand of Darcy's sound arm and sobbed quietly as a flurry of organised activity went on about her; the enormous relief she felt in that moment streamed down her face as tears. For days now, she had sat by Darcy's bedside, listened to the doctor's recommendations and hoped for a sign, just a small one, that her daughter was going to get better, that she was going to come back to her. Ever since the accident, she had gone over in her mind all the things she was going to do and say if Darcy recovered. Pippa was going to make the most of every moment they would be given, she just needed that chance.

'Mum,' Darcy's voice was very croaky.

'Yes, love,' Pippa said. 'I'm here, I'm right here.'

'Mum, what happened?' said Darcy. 'Why am I here?'

'Oh love,' Pippa was crying. 'You fell, you fell about twenty feet. It was the most awful thing. You broke your arm and hit your head. You've been unconscious for days, the doctors, they weren't sure you were ever going to wake up. Oh, Darcy, we've been so scared.'

Pippa buried her head in the sheets of Darcy's bed and cried as if her heart was breaking, the stress and worry finally released in an avalanche of emotion. Tom had finished talking with the doctors and moved to Darcy's bedside.

'Dad.'

Darcy smiled feebly up at him.

'How are you doing, sweetheart?' Tom asked.

He stroked her forehead.

'Dad, how did I fall? When?'

Darcy's questions were understandably confused, Tom waited patiently.

'The day we went to Tintagel to watch the eclipse, I was talking with David and your Mum, the next thing we knew, you had slipped down the cliff, we don't exactly know how you fell. I'm sorry.'

The next few days were filled with pulse checking, reviews of medical data and hospital food. Tom and Pippa would come and go, taking turns to sit by her side, keeping her amused with stories, reading to her and playing board games with her. On the third day after she regained consciousness, Darcy could leave her bed for the first time. Seven days after, she was on her way to the house that Tom had organised for them in Bude. A caravan park was no place for her to recover, so a friend of David's offered them the use of their holiday home.

'This is nice,' said Darcy as they walked through the front door.

The house reminded Darcy of the home in the hollow at Willow Wood. She smiled to herself.

'Oh, Kea,' she murmured.

Darcy spent a lot of time thinking about the events of the last few weeks. At one point, she felt she must have imagined the whole thing. Had it been a trick of her brain, a way of it coping with its injury? As she had thought more about it, though, she realised that this could not be the truth. The events that led to her injury had begun days before it. In fact, they were the cause of her accident, not caused by it. She thought about Mawgan and how she had seen him before going through the gateway into Dumnonia. When she had visited Jenna in the shop, she had called it mind twinning; a method of speaking mind to mind with another person without being together.

'Maybe that's what happened,' Darcy thought. 'Maybe I never really left, but my mind did.'

She thought about this more over the next few days as she felt stronger, more herself.

'It must be the truth,' she concluded.

In her mind, she had left through the gateway above the cliff face. She had jumped almost to her death and spent the next weeks unconscious in the hospital. She had gone, but she had also stayed. It was the only rational explanation, but then there was Jenna, Nix and Hicca, that did not explain them.

Darcy stood in the centre of the room. She was surrounded by her parents and their friends from the dig. She couldn't remember the last time she had a birthday party. It wasn't something her family had ever been big on. They were more the low-key celebration type, but Pippa had wanted to celebrate since Darcy's accident. It seemed important that they mark this passage of time. The lights in the room went out; her mother walked over with a cake lit by fourteen bright, multicoloured candles, and everyone sang.

'Happy Birthday to you; Happy Birthday to you...'

Darcy smiled, and on the ending of the song blew for all she was worth until every candle was out. Tom stood by the light switch and flicked it back on. In the nanosecond between darkness and light, Darcy found herself looking directly at the doorway to the room. She could have sworn he was there, Mawgan. It was only for an instant, but in that second, he was clearly visible. He smiled at her. Then he was gone. Darcy exhaled slowly, she was where she was meant to be, home, and it felt good.

EPILOGUE

Darcy had so many visitors over that week, she was feeling very loved and cosseted by the end of it. So much so that she was ready to suffocate. Friends of her parents from the Tintagel dig sent cards and 'get well' food by the bucket load. David often visited to see how she was doing. Darcy was feeling so much better that Pippa allowed her to go for a short walk around the town, just for some air, and also to escape the growing sense that Darcy would start climbing the walls soon if she couldn't get out of the house for at least a short while. Pippa was reluctant, but let Darcy go with the promise that she would be careful and not overdo it.

Walking down the high street, the buildings were as colourful as Darcy remembered them on the day she had been there with her mother, the day they had first found Tredinnick's Emporium. Darcy came to a stop outside the scruffy dark windows, looked upwards, and read the sign above the paint peeled door. Turning the handle, she went inside.

''Ello me dearie,' said a familiar voice.

Smiling, Darcy swung the door closed behind her.

Tom, Pippa and David sat on a scrap of rock at the excavation site in Tintagel. They looked through plans and drawings and observed the excavation techniques of the group of students from Exeter University who had come to help them for the summer.

'I think we'll take the baulk back a metre in the south corner,' David explained. 'That should uncover the rest of that feature Simon started digging yesterday.'

'Good idea,' Pippa agreed. 'Let's go give him the good news.'

The work was tough because of the hardness of the ground and the unrelenting heat from the sun. Simon, a young archaeology student, was busily excavating away the layers of fill in a feature he had begun to uncover the day before. He could see out of the corner of his eye Tom, Pippa and David making their way towards him. He chided himself for not being further along with his work so that he could give them some better evidence of what it was he was digging.

'Hi Simon, how goes it?'

Pippa called to him in her usual friendly manner, then she looked in his trench.

'Wow, that's really odd. Any ideas yet?'

'Not really,' said Simon. 'I'm just going to carry on and see what turns up further down.'

'What's that?'

David pointed to something that was just peeping out of the soil. It had a distinctive greenish tinge.

'It looks like it's copper alloy, whatever it is.'

Taking his trowel back out of his pocket, Simon proceeded carefully to pick around it, uncovering one small section at a time. The object slowly revealed itself. It was round with a glass casing and distinct pointers that whirled too quickly to read. They all marvelled at how perfectly preserved it appeared to be.

'It's some sort of pocket watch,' said David.

'No, I don't think so,' Pippa replied. 'Look at the hands, it's definitely not a watch.'

'It's a compass, it really is, just look at it.' said Tom.

They all stared at it for a moment, then at last Simon broke the silence.

'What's it doing here?'
David looked at Tom and Pippa, who shrugged back at him.
'I have absolutely no idea.' he said.